Kira's Kaleidoscope

A Holly Blue Bay Romance, Volume 2

Cathy Blossom

Published by Cathy Blossom, 2020.

Kira's Kaleidoscope
A Holly Blue Bay Romance
(Book 2)
By
Cathy Blossom
Copyright 2018 by Cathy Blossom
All rights reserved. No part of this publication may be reproduced in any form, electronically or mechanically without permission from the author.
This is a work of fiction and any resemblance to any person living or dead is purely coincidental.

This is a work of fiction. Similarities to real people, places, or events are entirely coincidental.

KIRA'S KALEIDOSCOPE

First edition. March 31, 2020.

Copyright © 2020 Cathy Blossom.

ISBN: 978-1393275237

Written by Cathy Blossom.

Chapter 1

KIRA

KIRA DAWSON POUNDED along the sand, trying desperately to catch her breath. Her heart was thumping loudly in her ears cutting out the sound of the sea lapping at the shore. Her lungs were screaming at her to stop, but she ignored the pain. She was going to complete this session. She was utterly determined to do so. Many people did this kind of exercise, and they loved it. She would do too, as soon as she stopped feeling like she was about to die.

Kira put her head down and continued jogging along the beach of Holly Blue Bay. Where was the rush of endorphins that people promised would happen? Where was the natural high that should be flowing through her? It should have happened by now according to all those health experts she followed online. Had they all been lying to her? She wouldn't put it past them. Their profile photos showed people who were far too happy. No one who jogged every day could look that happy.

Her thighs were starting to burn. They were probably in shock from all this unaccustomed exercise. How long had she been jogging now? Fifteen minutes? Twenty? It felt like an eternity. Kira checked the time on her phone. Four minutes! Was that all? That can't be right. She shouldn't feel this exhausted after running for four minutes.

She pressed her lips together. This just proved how unfit she was, and how taking up jogging was the right thing to do. Practise. That's what she had to do. Practise every day, and she'd soon be one of those grinning joggers who went out every day without fail and experienced that wonderful euphoria which came with running. Although, when she'd seen joggers out and about, they never looked happy. They looked more determined than happy.

She could do determined. So what if she couldn't breathe properly? And did it matter if her legs felt like jelly? It wouldn't be long before she had firm legs with defined muscles; legs that didn't jiggle and wiggle when she walked. And as for the sweat that was pouring off her, it probably made her look athletic. She nodded to herself and lifted her head higher. Yep, she must look like a professional jogger already. She kept that thought in mind as she forced herself across the sand looking left and right to see if anyone was giving her admiring glances for being so active.

Looking up had been a mistake. Her attention instinctively went to the ice cream kiosk to her left. Ben's ice cream kiosk. The small building where she went almost every day. The kiosk which contained the most delicious ice creams in the world. Not that she'd tasted all the ice creams in the world, but that didn't stop her from making that statement.

Ben, the owner of the kiosk and the maker of those amazing frozen desserts, spotted her and raised his hand in greeting. She could see his smile from here. People in the town often accused Ben of being the grumpiest person they'd ever met, but Kira never saw that side of him. He was always happy to see her. Which wasn't a surprise considering she was one of his most regular customers. He'd once joked that she should send a portion of her wages directly to him once a month, and Kira had seriously considered it.

But there wasn't going to be any ice cream today. Or this week. Possibly not ever again. She couldn't be eating calorie-laden treats if she was going to lose her excess weight. She'd read enough blogs to know that.

That sad thought made her steps slow down, and she was almost tempted to head to the kiosk and buy a small tub of strawberry ice cream to cheer herself up.

No. Those days were gone. She was a new person now. One who jogged every day. One who loved jogging every day! And one who never let ice cream pass her lips. Yes, this was the new Kira Dawson.

She gave Ben a quick wave before jogging away from him. She caught the confused look on his face, but there wasn't anything she could do about that at the moment. She couldn't stop mid-jog. If she stopped now, she would never get going again.

She set her attention on the lighthouse which was just over a mile away. She could do a mile. Of course she could. And once she got to the lighthouse, she would turn around and then jog the two miles back home. Then tomorrow, she would jog a bit further. That's what the experts told her; don't push yourself too hard when you first start out, but just hard enough.

Kira's steps slowed as she struggled to breathe. That blooming endorphin rush still hadn't appeared. Her vision blurred for a moment. Was she going to faint? Had she overdone it? She slowed down a bit more as she made her way towards the coastal path which led to the lighthouse. A second later, she stopped altogether and took a drink of water from her special jogger's bottle which she'd bought from Amazon the previous week. She used the edge of her special jogger's T-shirt to wipe the sweat off her forehead. She'd bought that from Amazon too.

Kira took another minute to allow her heart to calm down. She looked at her legs and raised her eyebrows in question at them. Could she jog for a bit longer? At least to the lighthouse? Her left knee began to shake as if giving her the answer.

Okay then. Not a jog, but she could definitely do a power walk. Her right knee began to shake at the thought. Not a power walk then, but definitely a stroll.

Kira took another long drink of water before strolling along the coastal path. A delightfully warm breeze caressed her sweating forehead. Kira quickly took a look around to make sure she was alone before raising her arms and letting the fresh air get to her armpits. She smiled. It felt good.

She continued to walk along the sandy path, gazing at the sea to her right as she did so. Despite living here all her life, the sight of the sea always lifted her heart. She was lucky to live in such a beautiful town. The gentle breeze seemed to agree with her thoughts and continued to cool her down.

Kira stopped at the bench in front of the lighthouse and collapsed onto it. This area gave one of the best views of Holly Blue Bay. You could see everything from here, including Ben's kiosk. There was a small line of people waiting to be served at the kiosk. Kira wished she was in that line too, and at the front.

A small, blue butterfly fluttered around a bush at her side. It was a holly blue butterfly, and the town had been named after these delightful creatures.

Kira sighed as she looked at the butterfly. It knew who it was, and what its purpose was in life. Even when it was a caterpillar, it knew what it was going to grow into, and what it would look like. How wonderful it must be to know without a doubt that you were exactly who you were meant to be, and nothing needed changing.

Kira rested a hand on her round stomach. She'd always been on the curvy side, and it had never bothered her. Until recently. There were a lot of changes going on in the town these days, and those changes had made Kira think about her life more.

Was she truly happy with her life? Should she get out more? Travel more? A few weeks ago, she'd discussed this with her colleague

Maureen at the library where they both worked. She had hoped Maureen would say Kira was fine just as she was.

But Maureen had given her a long look before saying, "Yes, you should definitely change. There's always room for improvement. You can start by getting out more and meeting a man."

Kira had argued that meeting a man wasn't going to change the feeling of restlessness she had about her life, but Maureen had said it would be a start. Then Kira had argued she didn't know how to meet a man. Ten minutes later, Maureen had Kira signed up to an online dating site. Ten minutes after that, nine men had been in touch asking to meet. Kira had been wary about their eagerness, but Maureen refused to listen to her excuses. Maureen deleted the time-wasters and told Kira she should at least give some of the men a chance. Mr Wonderful could be out there, Maureen had reasoned.

Kira had silently argued that Mr Weirdo could be out there too. Maureen had worn her down, and eventually, Kira had agreed to go on at least one date just to shut her up.

And this was why she'd started this ridiculous jogging regime. She couldn't meet anyone looking the way she did. She had to change. She had to be her best self, and that meant being thinner and fitter.

She looked again at the butterfly. "I bet you don't have these doubts about yourself, do you? You know how beautiful you are right from the moment you're born. I wish I felt like that. You don't need to make any changes to yourself, do you?" She paused. "Well, apart from changing from a caterpillar into a butterfly, of course. I think I'm still in the caterpillar stage, and I'm stuck in it."

Kira took her phone out and checked her messages. Since setting up her dating profile two weeks ago, she'd been in regular contact with a few men who seemed nice enough. They'd asked her out, but she hadn't said yes yet.

She took another look at the beautiful bay again. Things had to change. They couldn't stay the same forever. Change was good, if somewhat scary.

She made a decision and sent messages to two of the men she'd been messaging. She pressed send before she could talk herself out of it.

Then she stood up and had every intention of jogging back home. She jogged for ten seconds before her aching legs decided a walk would have to do. It was still exercise.

Kira was so lost in her thoughts that she didn't realise her treacherous feet had taken her in the wrong direction. Instead of taking her home, she'd ended up going in a different direction. But Kira didn't mind at all.

Chapter 2

BEN

BEN HAD STARED IN SURPRISE at Kira as she'd run along the beach earlier. He almost hadn't recognised her at first because he'd never seen her run before. Why was she running? Was someone chasing her? He'd looked at the area behind her ready to run over and rescue her from any would-be attacker. But no, there hadn't been anyone chasing her.

Ben had stared at Kira a bit more. Was she jogging? Actually jogging? He'd shaken his head in disbelief. Kira didn't do jogging. She was an intelligent woman. She wouldn't do something as daft as jogging. All that fast movement wouldn't do her digestive system any favours.

Even though she'd been a distance away, he'd seen how red her face was. But why was she putting herself through such an ordeal? Was she doing it for charity? Possibly. She was kind-hearted enough to do something like that. That must be it, he'd reckoned.

He was roughly brought out of his thoughts about Kira by a man at the front of the queue outside his kiosk.

The man snapped, "Are you listening to me, Ben? Did you hear what I said?"

Ben gave the man a disparaging look. "No, Ted, I didn't hear you. There's no need to shout. Your usual, is it?"

Ted tugged at his tight T-shirt and looked embarrassed. "Not today. The wife's got me on a diet. I was asking if you had any of that frozen yoghurt stuff. It's supposed to be better for you than ice cream; that's what the wife says."

Ben gave him a look which was colder than his choc ices. "Frozen yoghurt? Did I hear you right?"

Ted shifted to his other foot. "Yeah, frozen yoghurt. You can call it fro-yo too. That's what the wife told me."

"I don't care what you call it." Ben jerked his thumb to the board to his left. "Ted, can you read?"

"Course I can! There's no need to be rude. I was only ask—"

Ben interrupted him. "Can you read what's on this board? Can you see what I sell?"

"Yes, but—"

"Does it say anywhere on this board that I sell yoghurt, frozen or otherwise? Does it, Ted? Does it?"

Ted bristled. "There's no need to take that tone with me. I was only asking."

"You've been coming here for years. You know full well what I sell. You've tasted most of it."

Ted let out a small laugh. "Apart from the pistachio! I can't do with that at all."

Ben gave him a brisk nod. "Apart from the pistachio. Ted, if I had lost my mind and decided to sell frozen yoghurt for some absurd reason, don't you think I'd put it on my board? Hmm?"

"I suppose so," Ted muttered.

"And can you see it on my board?"

Ted looked at his feet. "No, I can't."

"Exactly. Which means I don't sell it."

Ted shot him a defiant look. "I was only asking in case you had some behind the counter. I don't know why I come here every day, I really don't. You're rude and obnoxious."

"I know," Ben replied. "If you don't want anything, then get out of the queue."

Ted hesitated. "I suppose I could have a small tub of ice cream. How many calories are in a small tub of vanilla?"

Ben gave him a long, hard look but didn't say a word.

Ted swallowed. "You don't know the answer to that. Okay. I don't either. I'll have the smallest tub of vanilla ice cream that you've got, please."

"Okay. Coming right up." Ben made to move away.

"And stick a chocolate flake in it," Ted called out. "The smallest one you've got."

"They only come in one size."

"Break it in two, give me half and you can have the other half," Ted suggested.

"I don't want half a flake."

Ted let out a resigned sigh full of martyrdom. "Okay, then I'll have it all. Put some of that chocolate sauce on too. And some of those crushed hazelnuts. Nuts are good for you."

"Anything else?" Ben asked.

Ted smiled. "No, that'll do. This is only a snack. I don't want to ruin my appetite for my lunch later." His smile faded along with the joy in his eyes. "I'm having a salad. The wife's making it for me. She's weighing everything out, and she's got me one of those smaller plates so my portion sizes aren't too large."

Ben gave Ted an uncharacteristic kind look as he handed the tub over. "Why's she doing that?"

Ted took the tub. "She wants me to change how I look." He shook his head sorrowfully. "It's because of all the changes that are going on in town. The wife said we'll have lots of tourists coming in, and she doesn't want them seeing me like this."

"There's nothing wrong with you."

"Try telling the wife that." Ted reached into his pocket.

Ben held his hand up. "It's on me, Ted. Enjoy it."

"Really? Thanks, Ben. The last meal of a condemned man, eh?" Ted's smile returned as he looked at the ice cream. He was still smiling as he walked away.

Ben quickly served the other people in the queue. Thankfully, there was no more silly talk of frozen yoghurt. His mind kept wandering back to Kira. He hoped she was okay. She should be here soon for her ice cream. He'd tell her about Ted and his diet. She'd have a laugh about that.

A cheery-faced young woman suddenly appeared in front of him. Ben wagged his finger at her and said, "You've got a lot to answer for, Daisy Clarke."

Daisy said, "What have I done now? Someone's always making complaints about me. Honestly, you wouldn't think I was here to improve the tourist trade, would you? People think I've made a pact with the devil, and that I want to destroy every aspect of Holly Blue Bay."

Ben explained, "Ted is on a diet. His wife wants him to change. She says she doesn't want all the new tourists to see him looking the way he is now."

Daisy frowned. "There's nothing wrong with him."

"I know. But he came here asking for frozen yoghurt."

"Did he? Why does he want that? You don't sell it. If you did, it would be on your board." She shook her head. "If people want frozen yoghurt why don't they buy it from the shop and then stick it in their freezers?"

"Some people are just plain crazy. Frozen yoghurt! Whatever next?" He studied her for a moment. "Are people giving you a hard time about the work you're doing?"

"Some of them." She shrugged. "But I can deal with it. I've been in marketing a long time, and I know things move slowly sometimes. People don't always like change. They'll see the benefit eventually when there's money coming into the town all year and not just in high season. Speaking of which, have you given any more thought to getting a website to showcase your marvellous wares?"

"I have given it some thought, and the answer's still no. Are you here for ice cream or to lecture me?"

Daisy laughed. "You're a stubborn one, Ben Roberts. But you're not the only stubborn person in this town." A blush came to her cheeks.

Ben gave her a rare smile. "Are you talking about our local handyman, Jacob? Aren't you two dating?"

"We are, as if you didn't know. The whole town knows about us. Jacob was resistant to change at first, but I'm working my marketing magic on him." She waggled her eyebrows. "He's even got a Facebook page now."

"He's gone to the dark side. But you're not going to drag me there. What can I get for you today?"

Daisy glanced at the board. "I'll have the strawberry surprise. What's the surprise?"

"You'll see when you get to the bottom." His mouth twitched. "But it won't be frozen yoghurt."

Daisy laughed. "Are you making a joke, Ben? I've never heard you make a joke before. All these changes in the air must be doing you good. Let me know when you're ready for your website. I'll help you set it up."

Ben shook his head at her. "You never give up, do you?" He handed her a cone full of strawberry ice cream.

"Never." She gave him a five-pound note. "Keep the change." She moved a short distance away before adding, "You need to move with the times, Ben. Perhaps you should sell frozen yoghurt." She broke into a grin and walked quickly away.

"Hey!" Ben called after her. He was about to say a lot more when Kira appeared at his kiosk. Her face was bright red, and she was gasping for air. "Kira! What's wrong?"

She put her hand on her waist. "I've got a stitch," she gasped. "I didn't know it could hurt so much."

"Don't move." Ben pulled his folding-up chair from under the counter, dashed outside and set the chair up for Kira. "Sit down and get your breath back."

"Thanks." Kira dropped into the chair.

Ben said to her, "Is it all that running you've been doing? I saw you earlier. I hope you're raising a good amount."

Kira gave him a quizzical look. "Raising a good amount? What do you mean?" She took a big drink of water.

"For the charity you're supporting. You must be running for a charity. Why else would you do it?"

Kira averted her gaze. "I was jogging for health reasons. I want to get fit."

"Hang on. You were jogging because you wanted to? No one was forcing you to do it?"

She looked back at him. "That's right. I jogged to the lighthouse. Well, some of the way. And I jogged back. Well, the last little bit."

Ben scratched his head. "Why?"

"Because I want to lose weight. I want to look different."

Ben groaned. "Not you too! What's got into everyone today?"

"There's nothing wrong with trying to improve yourself," Kira said primly.

Ben looked into her beautiful eyes and said truthfully, "You don't need to change anything. You're perfect just as you are."

"Oh! You have to say that. I'm the one who keeps you in profit." She cast a wistful look at his kiosk. "But I have to cut down on eating so much ice cream. You won't be seeing as much of me in future."

Ben quickly said, "You can still come here. I'm going to start selling frozen yoghurt. It's better for you than ice cream, apparently."

"Are you? Will it be low fat? And low calorie?"

"It will." He smiled at her. "You can test all the new flavours I come up with, like you do with the ice cream."

She smiled which made Ben's heart miss a beat. She said, "I'd like that. I don't suppose you've got a new flavour of ice cream you want me to try today? It is Saturday, and you usually have something delicious for me on a Saturday."

Ben smiled broadly at her. "I thought you weren't eating ice cream anymore."

She laughed. "It would be rude of me to refuse when you've gone to all this trouble of making a new flavour. I wasn't going to come here today, but my feet automatically brought me here. And now that I am here, I'm sure a small tub of ice cream won't hurt me." Her phone beeped and she looked at the message which had come through. She sighed. "Oh heck. I'm sorry, Ben, I'll have to say no after all."

"Why? What's wrong?" Ben was immediately concerned at the crestfallen look on her face.

"I have to go on a date tonight."

Ben wavered on his feet. "A date? A date with a man? Tonight?" Saying those words felt wrong in his mouth.

She nodded sadly. "This is all part of the new me. I'm going to get fitter and healthier, and I'm going to start dating. Maureen helped me set up an online dating profile."

"Maureen!" Ben said angrily. "What does she know? You shouldn't listen to her."

Kira winced as she got to her feet. "I know, but I did listen. And now I've agreed to go on a date." She looked straight into his eyes. "It's good to try new things, isn't it?"

Ben folded his arms. "Not if you don't want to. You don't look happy at the thought of going on a date."

"It's just nerves." She put her attention on her feet. "Ben, can I ask you an enormous favour?"

"Of course."

She looked back at him. "I'm meeting my date, Owen, at the Holly Blue Bay Hotel tonight. Could you be there too in case I need rescuing? If the date's a disaster, I'll be too polite to do anything about it. But you could. We could work out a secret signal if I'm in trouble, and you can rush in and rescue me like a knight in shining armour."

Ben couldn't say no to her. "I'll be your knight, but I'm not sure about the shining armour outfit. I'm right out of that."

Kira laughed and placed her hand on his arm. "What would I do without you? You're my best friend."

Ben managed to smile. Best friend? Of course. That's all they would ever be. But he'd rather be friends with Kira than not have her in his life. Seeing her on a date with another man was going to be torture. But he would do it.

Chapter 3

KIRA

KIRA PULLED AT THE hem of her dress as she walked into the Holly Blue Bay Hotel later that night. Her dress was too short and too tight. It had been a rash purchase last year, and was a size too small. She should have known better, but it wasn't the first time she'd bought something too small in the hope it would fit her one day. She had a special place in her wardrobe where she put such items. She called it her "some day" section. She tugged at the dress again. Wasn't the weight supposed to melt away now that she'd started jogging? That was the expression people used, wasn't it?

Well, nothing was melting away on her. The only thing that melted around her was Ben's ice cream. She smiled at that thought. She didn't know how Ben continued to perform such miracles with those concoctions of his. She was certain his new frozen yoghurt range would be just as delicious as his ice cream. Her nose scrunched up. Probably not quite as delicious, but a healthy alternative for a seasoned jogger like her.

A loud wolf whistle made her jump. She looked to where the noise had come from. Liza, the manager of the hotel, grinned as she looked Kira over. Liza said, "Look at you! That dress looks amazing on you. Get over here and let me have a proper look."

Kira grimaced as she walked over to the reception desk. "It's a bit short, and a bit tight. I should have worn something else."

"Nonsense. You look lovely. I wish I had your curves. I'm all sharp angles."

"I wish I was as tall and slim as you." She gave Liza a wry smile. "Perhaps I would be as slim if I didn't hang around Ben's kiosk all day."

Now that she couldn't have ice cream, Ben and his kiosk were constantly on Kira's mind. She glanced around her. Was he here yet? He had promised he'd be here, and Ben would never let her down.

Liza asked, "Are you looking for someone?"

"Yes. I'm on a date. I've booked a table. My date should be here soon."

"A date? Wow."

Kira put a hand on her stomach. "I feel sick with nerves. I shouldn't have agreed to do this."

"Why not? You're young and free. Why shouldn't you date? Is it someone I know?"

"No, I met him online. He's called Owen. He runs a food blog. He's big into healthy eating and exercise." Kira took a step closer and lowered her voice. "I lied a bit on my profile. I lied a lot actually. I said I was into health and fitness. I was hoping that if I wrote it down, it might come true. I even went jogging this morning."

"You didn't!"

Kira nodded. "I did. And I didn't have ice cream afterwards."

Liza frowned. "I bet Ben wasn't happy about that."

"I wasn't either." She looked towards the doors. "Have you seen Ben anywhere?"

"I thought your date was with a bloke called Owen."

"It is, but..." She trailed off. She didn't want to explain to Liza about how she'd asked Ben to look out for her. Now that she thought about it, it was a pathetic thing to do. She should be strong-minded enough to end a date if it wasn't going well.

Liza tapped her on the shoulder. "A very handsome man has just walked into the hotel. You can certainly tell he looks after himself. That is a very tight-fitting shirt he's wearing, and those jeans hug him very nicely indeed."

Kira looked towards the door and her stomach clenched with nerves. "It's Owen. He looks just like his profile photo." She gulped and added, "I don't look much like mine. I used a photo which was taken five years ago. I hope I don't scare him away."

"Don't be silly. You look a knockout. He's a lucky chap to be spending time with you."

Kira shot Liza a grateful smile before walking over to Owen. She gave him a shy smile and said, "Hi. I'm Kira."

Owen beamed at her showing perfect teeth. "Kira! Hi! You look amazing. Thanks for agreeing to meet me. I can't wait to get to know you better. I know we've got lots in common! I was so impressed by your profile and all the exercise you do! And you must tell me more about your diet. Do you really eat so much spinach every day?"

"Erm, yes." Kira gave him the most confident smile she could manage. She tried to recall exactly what she'd put on her profile.

Liza announced loudly, "Kira, would you like to go through to the dining room? Your waitress will be with you shortly."

Owen rubbed his hands together. "Great. I'm famished. I haven't eaten anything all day. But then you know why, don't you Kira?"

"I do?"

"Yes. You know the power of intermittent fasting. That's what you put on your profile. We must discuss that some more. I'm interested in your thoughts about it."

"Great. I can't wait." They headed into the dining room. The only fasting Kira did was when she was asleep. What on earth had possessed her to lie so much about herself?

They were shown to a table by the window which overlooked the bay. Kira took a seat and looked out of the window. She could see the lighthouse from here. It was hard to say if this view from the hotel was better than the view from the lighthouse. Both scenes were magnificent, and she knew how lucky she was to live here.

She turned to Owen who was studying the menu. "Owen, have you been to Holly Blue Bay before? You get a great view of it from here with the hotel being so high up."

Owen's brow furrowed as he continued to give his attention to the menu. He asked, "Where are the nutritional details listed? I'm used to seeing menus with all the nutritional values next to each dish." He turned the menu over as if expecting the information to be hiding there.

Kira shrugged. "They don't have them. I can tell you the food here is delicious. Especially the fish. It's caught fresh every day. If you look out of the window, you can see some of the fishing boats over there."

Owen tapped his chin while staring at the menu. "It's not my day for fish, I only eat it on Mondays and Thursdays. Where does the chicken come from? Is it organic?"

"I've no idea."

"What about the vegetables? Do they come from a sustainable source? What's the size of the suppliers' carbon footprint?"

"I really don't know. Look, the sun is starting to set. We'll get the full glory of it soon."

Owen scowled and finally looked at Kira. "I'll have to go with a plain salad. I can't risk ruining my diet with meat which comes from an unknown source. Are you going to have a salad too? We'll get it without dressing, of course."

Irritation flashed through Kira. "I'm not having a salad. I'm going to have the baked cod."

Owen gave her a nod. "I suppose a piece of plain cod would be okay. You can have that."

I can have it? Did he really just say that? Kira sat up straighter in her chair. "I'm going to have chips with it."

Owen laughed. "Yeah, right. You're so funny. You'll be telling me next you're going to have a glass of wine instead of water!"

Kira placed her hands on the table and gave Owen a firm look. "I am going to have a glass of wine. A big one."

Owen frowned and put his head to one side. "Are you sure about that? Perhaps a smaller glass would be better for you." Was it her imagination or did he glance at her stomach?

Kira gave him a tight smile. "I may very well have the whole bottle."

Owen burst out laughing. "I know what you're doing! You're trying one of those new diets out. Is it the one where you eat what you like one day, and then don't eat anything else for the next two days?"

"Almost."

The waitress came over, and Kira quickly gave her order. Owen took a lot longer because he quizzed the poor girl about the salad ingredients and wanted to know precisely where they had been grown. He even grilled her about who the supplier of the water was.

Once their order had been given, Owen continued to read the menu as if it were the most fascinating thing in the world. Kira knew she should start up a conversation, but she didn't know how to. She was beginning to feel annoyed with Owen and his obsession with the menu. Was it really that interesting? Perhaps it was to a food blogger.

Thankfully, it wasn't long before the food arrived. Kira licked her lips as her plate was put in front of her. Perhaps she was annoyed with Owen because she was so hungry. She'd soon feel better after eating a couple of chips. Maybe once they got chatting, Owen would turn out to be an interesting guy.

Kira picked a chip up and took a big bite. Yum. She shoved the rest of it in her mouth. She was feeling better already. She smiled at Owen and said, "Tell me more about yourself."

Owen was surveying his food silently.

"Is there something wrong with your meal?" Kira asked.

"No. I'm practising mindful eating." He glanced over at her. "I like to eat my meals in silence so that I can fully appreciate every morsel. You should do the same." His attention went back to his food. He reverently picked up a small tomato and placed it in his palm. He gazed at it in wonder and then slowly took a tiny bite of it. He closed his eyes as he slowly chewed.

Kira didn't know what to do or say. Should she make a break for it while his eyes were closed? But then she would waste her meal, and she didn't want to do that. She left Owen to his mindful eating and tucked into her fish. She turned slightly in her seat so she could appreciate the vista over the bay more. The sky was turning pale pink as the sun began its descent. There would be swathes of dark pink soon, followed by purples and then blues. She loved this time of day. She ate her wonderful meal, sipped the cold wine and gazed at the changing sky.

"I have finished," Owen loudly announced. Kira jumped. She'd forgotten he was there.

Kira looked at his plate and said, "You've left half of it."

Owen gave her a wise look. "The size of your plate shouldn't determine how much you should eat." He held his hand up. "I know when to say stop."

Kira looked down at her own plate. She would stop when her food was off the plate and in her stomach. She wasn't going to waste any of it.

Owen abruptly pushed his chair back and stood up. "I must leave you now. I like to stick to a night-time routine and I'll be beginning my wind-down practice soon. It was lovely to meet you, Kira. We must meet again. We've barely spoken to each other tonight."

Kira's eyebrows rose. It wasn't her who'd decided to be silent.

Owen continued, "I'll see to the bill on my way out."

"But we haven't had dessert yet."

Owen chuckled. "Dessert! You are too funny. On our next date, I'll take you to a vegetarian café I know. You'll love it. It's amazing. They have over one hundred different kinds of seeds and nuts."

Kira knew this was the perfect time to tell him there wouldn't be a second date, but she was too much of a coward to do so. She'd do it by text later. To alleviate her guilt about that, she said, "I insist on paying for the meal. I may find a small corner or two for a bit of dessert yet. They do a wonderful sticky toffee pudding here."

Owen tapped the side of his nose as if they were sharing a secret. "I understand. Stuff your face today, and fast tomorrow." He gave her another perfect smile before walking away.

Kira watched him with a sinking heart. Owen would be the perfect man for someone, but not her. She picked up the dessert menu even though she'd already decided on the sticky toffee pudding. She liked reading the descriptions of the desserts. She jumped as Ben suddenly sat down in Owen's seat.

"Crikey! Where did you come from?"

"I've been sitting in a dark corner in the lounge," Ben said. "I've been here all night." His face twisted in disgust. "That date of yours didn't hang around long. Are you going to see him again?"

"No. He's not my type."

Ben let out the loudest sigh of relief that Kira had ever heard. He leaned back in his seat. "Do you want a lift home? It's starting to get dark, and I don't want you walking home in the dark. And there's no point in you getting a taxi when I've got my car outside."

She smiled at him. "A lift would be great, thanks. But I'm having some dessert first. Do you want some?"

Ben shifted in his seat and placed his hands on the table. There was a twinkle of mischief in his eyes which Kira had never seen before. He said, "How would you like to go somewhere where you can eat all the ice cream you can manage? And you don't have to pay for any of it."

Kira put the dessert menu down, stood up and said, "I'll just settle the bill."

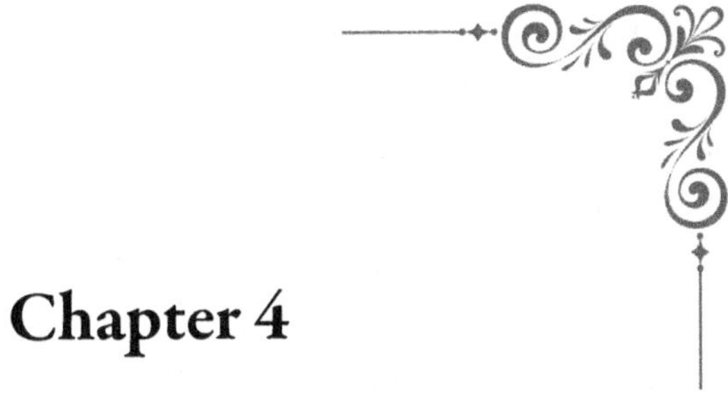

Chapter 4

BEN

AS BEN DROVE ALONG, he cast a sideways glance at Kira in the passenger seat. She was staring glumly out of the window.

"Hey, what's wrong?" he asked. "Your face is all scrunched up."

She looked his way. "I am an awful person. You should take me home, chuck me out of your car and refuse to have anything else to do with me."

"Oh? Have you killed someone?"

"No. Don't be silly."

"Well, what have you done that's so awful?"

Kira sighed. "I told lies about myself online. I made things up when I was doing my dating profile. I misled people. I wrote terrible lies about myself."

Ben tried not to smile at her serious expression. "What kind of lies? Did you tell people you're an astronaut? An ice-skating champion? A horse whisperer?"

Kira's eyes widened. "No! I didn't tell them anything like that." A tiny smile came to her face. "You are being very silly, Ben. This is a serious matter. I'm trying to confess my sins to you."

Ben gave her a solemn nod. "Go ahead. Confess."

Kira took her phone out and scrolled through it. "I said I was a fitness fanatic."

"That's not a lie, you did go jogging this morning."

"Yes, but I put a list of activities I apparently enjoy on a regular basis." She continued to scroll down. "It's a long list. I wrote that I'm an expert at scuba diving. I often run marathons, sometimes just for fun. I'm a black belt in karate. In between those activities, I do a lot of cycling, often twenty miles in a morning. Oh, and I'm an expert at ice skating. You were right about that."

Ben burst out laughing. "Why did you put all those things on your profile?"

She shrugged. "I don't know. I wrote what I really like doing first like reading and watching movies, but it sounded so boring. I decided to liven it up a bit. I did get carried away somewhat. But that's not all. I made a list of the food which I eat, things like salads, fruit, veg, organic stuff. All the things people tell you to eat. None of it is true, of course. And that's why Owen contacted me. He thought we were a good match. But we weren't. I deceived him and wasted his time."

Ben cast a soft look her way. "Owen was lucky to spend time with you. By the way, why was he eating with his eyes closed?"

"He was practising mindful eating."

"What?"

"It's a way of enjoying your food more."

Ben shook his head. "The world is a mysterious place full of strange people. Kira, don't feel bad about your dating profile. From what I've heard about this dating thing, lots of people lie about themselves."

"Yes, but there are little lies, and there are whopping big lies like I told. I shouldn't have done it. Poor Owen. The least I can do is phone him tomorrow and tell him the truth. I hope he's a forgiving person." She put her phone away and stared at her knees.

Ben didn't like to see her looking so upset. "Kira, look at the cows in that field over there. The farmer is bringing them in for the night."

Kira frowned as she looked that way. "I can see them. What's so special about them?"

"Those are the cows who supply the milk I use for my ice cream. I like to have my raw materials nearby." He turned into a road on the right. "And this is where I live."

Kira stared at the buildings ahead of them. "You live on a farm? I didn't know that."

"I live in a building at the back of the farm." He drove along the road, past the farm buildings and around the corner. He parked in front of a huge barn which had a sign on the top of it.

Kira's mouth dropped open. "You live in that massive building? Why have you got such a huge sign for your name? Do you keep forgetting what you're called?"

Ben switched the engine off. "That's the name of my company."

Kira turned her confused face to him. "Your company? I thought you only ran that kiosk on the beach."

"I make a lot of ice cream for other businesses in town too. Also, in exchange for a low price on the milk, I give the farmer here a good deal on the ice cream that he sells in his farm shop."

"There's a farm shop? Where? What does it sell?" She gave him a direct look. "Where else does your ice cream go?"

"I supply ice cream to Liza's hotel, and to the ice cream parlour in town." He brushed a bit of fluff from his jeans. "I actually own the ice cream parlour."

"What!" Kira screeched. She freed herself from her seat belt and twisted around in her seat to look at him better. "Ben Roberts! You've been keeping a lot from me. Why didn't I know about all this?" She waved her hand at the building in front of them. "We've been friends for years. We talk all the time. Why haven't you told me about your ice cream empire?"

He shrugged. "The subject never came up."

Kira gave him a long, searching look. "You should have brought the subject up. Why didn't you? Did you think I'd only talk to you because you owned a thriving business? Did you think I was that shallow?"

Ben shrugged again. He had dated women who were only interested in his thriving business, but he wasn't going to tell Kira that.

"Ben, you don't have to keep secrets from me. I won't tell anyone that you're an entrepreneur, if that's what you are."

Ben said, "I didn't mean to keep it a secret. It isn't one anyway, not to my suppliers. Or my employees."

"You have employees?" Kira rolled her eyes. "Of course, you have employees. You can hardly run a business this size on your own. You are a man of mystery. What else have you been keeping from me?"

"Nothing else," Ben lied. He certainly wasn't going to reveal how he truly felt about her. "Would you like to go inside?"

"Inside your ice cream factory? Of course I would. Where's the front door?" Kira flung the passenger door open and got out.

Ben smiled to himself, got out of the car and walked over to her. He explained, "I can't take you into the main factory because of health and safety reasons. Everyone who goes in has to have certain hygiene requirements and whatnot."

Kira nodded. "That's understandable." She gave him a gentle prod in his chest. "If you've only brought me here to show me this building and then to tell me I can't go in, our friendship is over, Mr Roberts." The twinkle in her eyes belied her words.

Ben shoved his hands in his pocket. "I've got a little cottage behind this building. I had it extended to include an experimental kitchen. It's where I come up with new ideas. There's everything I need in the kitchen like fruit, sauces, nuts, chocolate, of course. Would you like to come in the kitchen with me and make your own ice cream? You can use whatever you want. And you can eat as much as you like."

Kira's eyes were as wide as saucers. "Until this moment, I had no idea you were the perfect man, Ben. I may have to marry you."

Even though he knew she was joking, he still enjoyed the warm and tingly feeling which washed over him at Kira's words. He would replay them many times in the future, particularly on those days when he had irritating customers to deal with. Which was every day.

Kira said, "I don't understand why you run the kiosk. You obviously don't have to. You could get someone to do it for you."

"I like being there." He stopped talking and nodded in the direction of the building. "Shall we?" As well as never telling Kira how he really felt about her, he would never tell her the real reason why he worked at the kiosk on the beach.

Chapter 5

KIRA

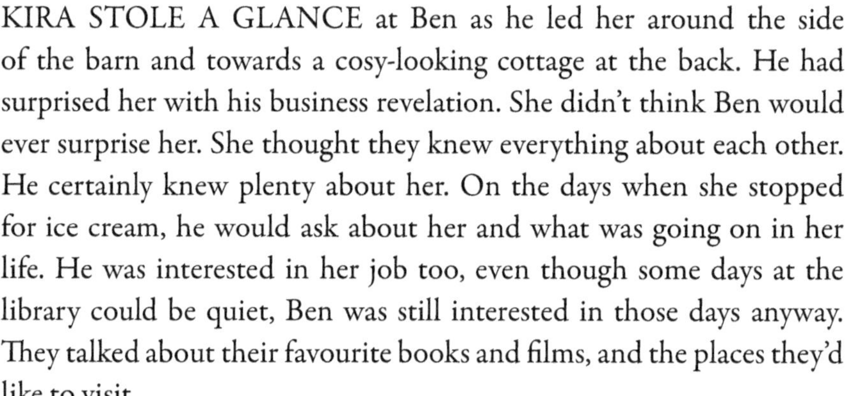

KIRA STOLE A GLANCE at Ben as he led her around the side of the barn and towards a cosy-looking cottage at the back. He had surprised her with his business revelation. She didn't think Ben would ever surprise her. She thought they knew everything about each other. He certainly knew plenty about her. On the days when she stopped for ice cream, he would ask about her and what was going on in her life. He was interested in her job too, even though some days at the library could be quiet, Ben was still interested in those days anyway. They talked about their favourite books and films, and the places they'd like to visit.

Kira frowned at her thoughts. Had it been Ben who'd asked all the questions? Had she poured forth every detail of her life while he gave barely anything in return? Had he only been listening to her out of politeness? After all, he'd been like a trapped prisoner in that kiosk while she'd rambled on incessantly.

Ben nudged her. "What's wrong now? Your face is doing that scrunched-up thing again."

"Ben, have I bored you over the years? When I came to your kiosk, did you listen to me just to be polite?"

Ben stopped in his tracks. "Absolutely not. I loved talking to you."

"I feel it was all one-sided, our friendship. Was it?" She looked at his kind face, a face she knew well.

"It wasn't. I told you things too. And you did me a favour by bringing books from the library for me. Don't forget the sandwiches too. You brought me plenty of those. And you still do."

"I call in the sandwich shop all the time, so it's no trouble to get you something. Are you sure I haven't bored you over the years?"

Ben gave her a searching look. "I'm sure. You're having some strange thoughts tonight. I blame that jogging. It did something to your brain."

"It probably did. Sorry for being all serious. I'm feeling a bit weird, not quite myself. And I don't know what to do about it."

"I know something you can do." He opened the front door of the cottage, stood to one side and said, "After you. You can hang your coat and bag up in the hall."

Kira stepped into the cottage. She caught the aroma of vanilla in the air. She hung her coat and handbag on the stand in the hall and then followed Ben into the charming living room. There was a big, open fire beneath a solid-looking mantelpiece. A sofa was opposite the fire and it had those big, comfy cushions which looked so inviting. Kira could just imagine herself sinking into the sofa and not moving for hours. She noted the bookshelves and saw how packed they were.

She gave Ben an accusing look. "Why did you need to borrow so many library books if you've got all of those?"

"I've read those ones. Besides, I like to support the local library. Follow me into the kitchen."

Kira did so. Considering how the living room was decorated, she was expecting the kitchen to be of a typical country style. But it wasn't.

"Wow!" She exclaimed. "Look at this place! It's so shiny and high-tech. There's so much metal. I was expecting a big wooden table and a dresser." She moved further into the kitchen and slowly turned around. "This is the last kitchen I would expect you to have, Ben." She stopped turning. "But I'm beginning to realise I don't know the real you at all."

Ben said gruffly, "You know me better than anyone else. What do you want to make first? I've got some tubs of vanilla ice cream in freezer number one. We can use that as a base, or we could make a batch of ice cream from scratch. I've got a machine over there which will do that in less than thirty minutes. I've got a cupboard full of ingredients you can add to the ice cream such as fruit, biscuits, nuts, chocolate in many shapes and sizes. Then there's the fresh produce in the fridge along with the fruit sauces. I've got some alcohol in that cupboard over there if you want to make a more grown-up ice cream. The usual like rum, vodka, gin—"

Kira held her hands up. "Stop! That's too much information. Hang on, you said freezer number one. How many freezers have you got in here?"

"Just four. I've got over a hundred in the factory barn."

"Okay. Let me just process that information first." She shook her head. "I've forgotten what you said after freezer number one. Can you start again?"

"I'll show you instead. You can use anything in ice cream. I've made some with caramelized brown bread, Christmas pudding, even a bacon one! That was surprisingly delicious." He gave her a serious look. "My biggest mistake was a salmon and dill ice cream. It was horrendous. I still have nightmares about that, and indigestion."

Kira smiled. "I won't use salmon."

She followed Ben around the amazing kitchen. She noticed how animated he was as he spoke about the ice cream. She hadn't realised it was such a passion with him. She felt guilty all over again about how little she knew about him. No matter what Ben said, she was sure their conversations at the kiosk had been more about her life than his. Well, she could do something about that.

"Ben, why do you like ice cream so much? Is it a family thing?"

"Not at all." He led her over to the steel-topped table and pulled a chair out for her. He sat down and indicated for Kira to do the same. He began, "When I was growing up, I always thought ice cream was a treat, and one that you had now and again."

Kira nodded. She didn't want to interrupt Ben by adding her own opinions about ice cream. This was a time to listen, and not to talk about herself.

Ben continued, "I came to this town with my family when I was nine years old. We didn't have a lot of money, but Mum and Dad saved up all year so we could have a few days out. And on those days out, they would buy us treats." He smiled at the memories. "They weren't huge treats really, but they were to me and my brother."

"Your brother? What's his name?"

"Gordon. He's a few years younger than me. He's the clumsiest person I've ever met. He constantly trips over fresh air. Anyway, Mum and Dad took us to a kiosk on the beach for an ice cream."

"Your kiosk?" Kira pulled a face. "Sorry, I keep interrupting."

"That's okay. Yes, the very same kiosk. I remember everything about seeing that kiosk for the first time. Mum bought Gordon and me an ice cream. I had strawberry, and Gordon had chocolate. We both had raspberry sauce on it, and those little sprinkles. Well, you know about the sprinkles. I put them on your ice creams all the time."

Kira's cheeks warmed up at the kind smile Ben was giving her. Had his smile always been that kind?

Ben said, "We walked away from the kiosk, and two seconds later, Gordon tripped and dropped his ice cream. He cried so loudly that he scared the seagulls away. I saw Mum scrabbling about in her purse trying to find more money, but I knew she didn't have much to share. So I gave Gordon my ice cream."

Kira's eyes began to sting at the thought of a little Ben giving his ice cream away.

"I stayed right by Gordon's side to make sure he didn't move and drop his second ice cream," Ben said with a smile. "You should have seen how happy he was as he started to gobble it up."

"That was kind of you. Did Gordon share it with you?"

Ben's nose wrinkled in disgust. "No, and I didn't want him to. He was a very messy eater. He didn't need to share because the kind woman in the kiosk saw what had happened and she came over to me with a free ice cream. Mum tried to pay, but the woman wouldn't let her. Estelle, she was called. The ice cream woman, not Mum." Ben stood up. "It wasn't just a normal ice cream. It was a magical one. I can't really explain what I mean. I'll have to show you instead. Come with me."

Kira went with Ben over to a cupboard. He pulled it open and said, "This is where I keep my ice cream cones. The one Estelle gave me was a double one like this." He reached into a box and took a cone out. "Here, hold this."

Kira took the cone. "I am familiar with this size," she told him solemnly. "As you know."

Ben smiled before moving to a large freezer. He opened it up and grabbed several tubs. He put them on the table and then moved over to other parts of the kitchen to collect other ingredients.

When he'd got everything he needed, he said to Kira, "Hold your cornet up. Don't drop it. It's going to get heavy."

Kira did as she was told. She was finding it hard to tear her gaze away from Ben. He looked so alive and full of joy.

Ben scooped some ice cream into the cornet. "Estelle started with vanilla. Then she added mint, followed by chocolate. Like this." He scooped generous amounts into both sides of the cornet. "Then she added rhubarb ice cream. It's delicious. Followed by coconut and hazelnut flavoured ones. After that came the toppings." Ben covered the ice cream in three flavours of sauce. Tiny pink and white marshmallows were added along with multi-coloured sprinkles and chocolate chips.

Kira had to keep swallowing the saliva in her mouth. She was going to start drooling if she wasn't careful.

Ben said, "The finishing touch was a crunchy sherbet made in all the colours of the rainbow. It had glitter in it too which caught the sun and made my ice cream sparkle." His face was aglow at the memory. He sprinkled sherbet over the top of the amazing ice cream which was now making Kira's hand drop. "Now, imagine you're a child and you're given this. It was the most magical thing I'd ever seen. I was certain Estelle must have been a wizard to create such a thing. Kira, you'd better eat it. It's starting to melt."

Kira stared at the amazing creation. "I don't think I can. It's too beautiful."

Ben nodded in understanding. "That's what I thought. For days after Estelle gave me this ice cream, I couldn't stop thinking about it. I became obsessed with making my own ice cream. The best part of working at the kiosk is seeing the look on children's faces when I give them something like this. Obviously not as big as that one you're holding. I don't want to overload them with sugar. But Kira, you should see how happy they are."

"Do they look as happy as me?" She gave him a huge grin. "Would you like to share this with me? I don't like to admit defeat, but I can't manage all of this."

"Let me get some bowls and we'll eat it that way. And after that, we can make some ice cream for you to take home." He turned away from her and headed for a drawer.

Kira couldn't speak. This was a totally different side of Ben, but still comfortingly familiar. She was aware of her phone beeping in her pocket, but she didn't answer it. She didn't want to ruin this evening with Ben.

It was hours later when Kira looked at her phone. Ben had driven her home after they'd made three tubs of ice cream. Kira had told him her tiny fridge would only hold two, so he'd agreed to keep the other one at his place for now.

As Kira read the message on her phone, she groaned in despair. When she'd agreed to meet Owen for a date, she'd also contacted a man called Joe and had agreed to meet him too. He'd replied during this evening and said he'd meet her first thing tomorrow for a stroll and a chat in the park.

Kira was tempted to cancel, but she didn't want to let Joe down. He seemed like a nice guy, another one whom she'd misled with her lies. She would meet him tomorrow and explain what she'd done. She hoped he'd understand.

Chapter 6

BEN

EVEN THOUGH IT WAS Sunday morning, Ben liked to get up early so he could deliver some of his ice cream orders to local businesses. He did have delivery drivers who did this for him, but he still liked to be part of this process.

He was heading away from town after his last delivery when he decided to go for a walk in the park. It was a sunny morning, and it was early enough for the park to be relatively empty. He wanted time to process his thoughts about Kira. He'd been thinking about her all night. He'd never invited a woman to his home before, and he'd never asked them to make ice cream with him. He chuckled to himself as he recalled Kira's scrunched-up face as she stared at all the ingredients she could put in her ice cream. In the end, she'd packed her tubs with as many different ingredients as she could fit in. Ben wasn't sure how the ice creams would taste, but Kira had assured him they would be wonderful.

Ben parked the delivery van outside the park and walked casually towards the gates. An impossible thought came to his mind; could he ask Kira out on a date? A proper date? His shoulders sagged as he entered the park. But what if she said no? What if she was embarrassed and never came to his kiosk ever again? That would be awful. No, he couldn't take the chance of that happening. It was too risky. They would have to stay friends; it was safer that way.

Ben was so lost in his thoughts that he almost didn't hear the whimper coming from a woman slumped on a bench near the entrance. The red-faced woman lifted a shaking arm and groaned at him.

Ben ducked his head and gave her a wide berth. It was probably someone who had been out drinking all night, possibly on a hen party or something. Ben pursed his lips in disgust. Why couldn't people take better care of themselves when they were out drinking? Holly Blue Bay was not the kind of town which welcomed such behaviour and most drinking places closed before midnight.

The woman groaned again and called out, "Ben. Help."

Ben came to a sudden stop. That was Kira's voice. He spun around and dashed over to the slumped figure. He knelt at Kira's side. Her face was as red as a tomato. Her eyes were full of anguish, and she waved her hand feebly in the air.

"Kira? What's wrong with you? What's happened? Have you been out all night drinking? That's not like you. Did you get so drunk you forgot where you lived?"

Kira frowned at him. "So drunk I forgot where I lived? Ben, what are you talking about? Do I look as if I've been here all night?"

Ben cast a glance at the clothes she was wearing. "You've got your pyjamas on. Have you been sleepwalking?"

Kira made an effort to sit up straighter, grimaced and then slumped back on the bench. "These are my casual weekend clothes. They're designer ones. I got them on eBay. Can you help me sit up, please?"

"Of course." Ben sat on the bench and pulled Kira into a sitting position. She leaned against him which didn't bother him at all. He looked down at her and asked, "Have you been jogging again?"

"It's worse than that." She shook her head at herself. "Ouch! Even moving my head hurts. I've been on a date."

Ben's heart sank. "A date? Another one? With that same man again? Oscar or Oliver? Whatever his name was." Ben knew full well what the man's name was.

"No, not him. It was Joe this time. I sent a message to him yesterday morning and agreed to go on a date. I wasn't thinking straight when I sent that message; I can see that now. Anyway, he wanted to meet me at this park for a chat and a stroll around. I liked the idea of strolling so I said yes."

"I like the idea of strolling too," Ben agreed. "You can see a lot more when you stroll."

Kira went on, "Because of my online lies, Joe was under the impression I was a fitness freak, and I wanted to tell him the truth about myself in person. It seemed the right thing to do. So, when he said he'd like to meet me, I said yes. I thought we could have a little walk while I told him what an awful person I was."

"You're not an awful person," Ben interjected. "I don't know why you have to put yourself down so much."

Kira let out a sigh. "I know, but it's a habit I suppose. Anyway, when I got here, Joe met me at the gates and said we should start with a walk to warm up. Warm up to what? I thought, but I just went along with it. Our warm-up walk turned into a jog, then a run and then a sprint. I kept trying to tell Joe I wanted to talk, but he said we'd talk once we'd finished our routine."

"You should have turned around and left. This Joe fella sounds like a rude and self-centred sort of person if you ask me. Is he still here? I'll tell him what I think about him."

"No, he's gone. Along with the rest of his boot-camp buddies."

Ben's eyes widened. "What do you mean by that?"

Kira gave him a smile. "I thought the sprinting part was bad enough, but Joe took me over to the playing fields at the far end of the park. I never go over there because it's where serious activity goes on."

Ben nodded. "I know, I've seen folk there. Playing football matches and netball. Even cricket sometimes. I don't know what gets into people sometimes."

"Me neither. Joe took me to a group of people over there. They go to a boot camp that he runs, and he thought it would be fun if I met them. The people were those athletic types who can jog on the spot and talk at the same time. I would have turned around and run away, but my legs had almost given up on me at that point." She gently patted her legs. "Poor legs. I'm so sorry for putting you through this."

"What happened with the boot camp people?"

Kira shivered. "There were many, many exercises. I don't know the names of some of them. There were squats and lunges, press-ups and star jumps. It was awful, Ben. I did my best to keep up, but I failed miserably. The others didn't even break into a sweat. And once they'd finished those awful exercises, they went on a five-mile run around the park to cool down. Cool down? Can you believe it?"

"You poor thing. I'm sorry you had to go through that."

"Me too." Kira leaned her head on his shoulder. "Ben, I tried to make it to the gates, but my legs have well and truly given up on me. Would you mind sitting with me while I recover? If I recover?" She leaned against him a bit more.

Ben's arm suddenly had a mind of its own and it sneakily put itself around Kira's shoulders. Kira didn't seem to mind, so he left it there. He said, "Do you need to be somewhere?"

"Only home. All through my ordeal, I kept thinking about that ice cream we made last night. I thought that as soon as I get home, I'm going to eat a full tub. I'll have to eat something to get my strength back. I must have burned three million calories this morning."

"Maybe more," Ben added. He cleared his throat. "So, are you going to see this Joe person again?"

"No. But he was the one who decided we weren't compatible. I think he realised that when I collapsed for the fifth time on the playing field gasping for air. He seemed fine about it, so at least I didn't have to admit how much I'd lied. Although, he's probably worked out I'm not a fitness nut." She turned her head and looked at Ben. "I don't want to talk about Joe or anyone else. I'm giving up on dating for now. It's more trouble than it's worth."

Ben gave her a small smile. He wasn't sure if he was pleased or not at her comments. He didn't like the idea of her dating other men, but he still didn't want to risk their relationship by putting himself forward as a possible suitor considering what she had just told him. A fine pickle he was in.

He said to Kira, "My van's parked outside the gates. Would you like a lift home?"

"Yes, please." She stared intently at her legs, and her face turned red with effort. "Erm, we have a problem. I'm trying to move my legs but they're not responding. I think they've gone to sleep or they're on strike. I'll just have to stay here until I feel better. You don't have to stay with me."

Without fully realising what he was doing, Ben swiftly got to his feet, scooped Kira into his arms and announced, "I will carry you to the van. I can't leave you here in this condition."

"Don't put your back out," Kira said as she put her arm around his shoulders.

"You're as light as a feather."

"Yeah, right. A huge feather which weighs a ton."

Ben gave Kira a serious look. "Stop talking about yourself like that. Would you let anyone else talk to you like that?"

Kira glanced to the side. "No, I don't suppose so."

"Well then." Ben strode towards the gates carrying his precious cargo. Kira did feel light in his arms, but that could be because having her there made him feel as if he was walking on air. He suddenly wished he'd parked his van miles away.

He smiled down at Kira, and she smiled back at him. He was so glad he'd decided to go for a walk in the park. It had been a short walk, but look how wonderfully it had ended.

Chapter 7

KIRA

KIRA HAD NEVER BEEN carried in anyone's arms before. Well, she must have been carried about by Mum and Dad when she was little, but no one had scooped her into their arms like Ben had done. And so easily too. He must have hurt himself doing that. She pressed her lips together and stopped her self-deprecating thoughts from continuing. Ben was right; she did put herself down a lot. She would make a conscious effort to stop doing that.

She stole a glance at Ben's face. He was smiling as if he were happy to carry her along like this. He was a good friend. She wasn't sure anyone else would have rescued her from the park. They would have left her there, or if they had decided to rescue her, they would have needed a wheelbarrow to move her.

Stop that horrible thought, she chided herself.

Ben took her over to his van and opened the passenger door. "Mind your head," he told her as he slid her carefully onto the passenger seat. He was so gentle and treated her like she was a valuable object. He asked, "Can you manage the seat belt or should I do it for you?"

"My arms haven't given up on me yet, so I'll do it myself. Thanks, Ben, for not leaving me in the park."

"It's no problem." He gave her a warm smile. He had a lovely smile. Kira had never noticed how lovely his smile was before. But there were a lot of things she was noticing about Ben these days.

Ben made sure she was buckled up before he drove away. The radio came on and he began to sing along.

Kira said, "You've got a lovely voice, all deep and mellow. You should join the church choir."

"No, thanks. I see enough of the people around here without mixing with them on a Sunday." He shot her a grin. "And don't you be telling Reverend Pendleton I've got a good voice. If he asks me to join the choir, I wouldn't be able to say no to him. You know what that sneaky man of the cloth looks like when he asks you a favour. All big-eyed and pleading like a puppy. It's impossible to say no to the man, and he knows it."

Kira laughed. "You're right about that. Perhaps it's part of his training. He's used that look on me many times. I've been to hundreds of charity events at the church hall because of that look. But what can you do? You have to say yes to Reverend Pendleton. It's just a fact of life."

Ben let out a loud laugh. "We should put that on a car bumper sticker."

They continued to chat about people in Holly Blue Bay, and then the events they'd been to over the years. Their talk turned to the work Daisy Clarke was doing for the town.

Kira said, "You might have to get a bigger kiosk to deal with all the extra tourists that are going to come into town."

"I hope not. I've got enough on my hands with the residents here." He stopped outside her house. "Shall I help you inside?"

Kira took her seat belt off. "No, I'll be fine. I'm feeling much better now." She opened the door and moved forward fully expecting her legs to move. They didn't and she slid out of the seat and onto the pavement. It took her by surprise and she sat there staring at the pavement as if wondering where it had come from.

Before she knew it, Ben was sweeping her into his arms again. He was laughing. "Are you hurt?"

"No, just embarrassed." She looked towards her neighbour's house. "If anyone's watching me, they'll think I'm drunk. First, I couldn't get off that park bench, and now I can't walk to my front door." She looked at Ben's mirth-filled face. "Hey, this is a serious matter. My reputation is at stake here."

"Who cares what the neighbours think?" He strode towards her door. "Who cares what anyone thinks? I don't."

"That must be a nice way to live," Kira said wistfully.

Ben stopped at her front door. "It's the only way to live. Let's give the neighbours something to talk about. Open your door, and I'll carry you across the threshold. We'll look like a pair of happy newly-weds."

"You're a wicked man, Ben," Kira said with a smile. She pulled her keys from her pocket and opened the door. Ben carried her inside. She found to her surprise that she didn't mind at all if the neighbours thought they were newly-weds.

Ben closed the door with his foot and said, "Now where?"

"Into the living room, please. You can put me on the sofa." She pointed the way to the living room.

"Will do." Ben walked that way and gently placed her on the sofa. Then he took a step back and cast an admiring look around the room. "I like what you've done in here. It's modern, but not too modern. Very cosy and inviting." He broke into a broad smile as he looked at the shelves. "We've got the same taste in books. And films." He moved over to some travel posters. "Are these the places you've been to?"

"Not yet. But I want to go someday. I like to have visual reminders of places I want to go, or things I want to have in my life." She hesitated, unsure of whether to continue. But it was Ben, and she could tell him anything. She retrieved a large book from the table in front of her. "This is my vision book."

"Pardon? Your vision book? What's one of those?"

"Sit down and I'll tell you. But don't you dare make fun of me."

"I would never do that." Ben sat down and gave her an earnest look. "Unless it's something so ridiculous that I have to make fun of it."

She gave him a gentle whack on the arm. "If that happens, you'll have to give me free ice cream for the rest of my life."

"Okay, I will. Let's have a look at this vision book, then."

Kira opened the book. "I read about this online, and how you're supposed to make pictures of things you want in your life. I thought it was a load of nonsense at the time, but I decided to try it." She tapped the first page. "Look, I wanted a certain sofa for this room and so I cut out pictures of ones I really liked." She smiled at the top photo on the page. "And that's the one we're sitting on now. I got it for half price."

"That's just a coincidence."

"Do I detect a scoffing tone in your voice?"

Ben shrugged. "I'm reserving judgement until you show me the rest of the book."

Kira turned another page and pointed to certain items. "I got that from a jumble sale at the church. And I got that from Mary next door. She didn't need it anymore."

Ben gave her a sideways look.

Kira said, "It doesn't work all the time, but it's great when it does. I've got pictures of the holidays I want to go on. Do you want to have a look, or do you still think I'm being silly?"

"I never said you were silly. Let's see where you want to go."

Kira turned the page. "I'd like to go to Edinburgh one day. I know it's not far away, but I've never been. I'd love to visit the castle and go on one on those tour buses." She stopped talking. "Ben? What's wrong? You've got a funny look on your face."

"You're not going to believe this, but my brother has an apartment in Edinburgh. He's overseas with work for a few months, and he said I could stay there whenever I want. He even sent me a spare set of keys." A kind look came into his eyes which sent a warm feeling washing through Kira and quite surprised her. Ben continued, "You are more than welcome to stay there. It's a two-bedroom apartment, so you could take a friend if you wanted."

Kira couldn't speak for a moment. "Really? I could do that? I should pay your brother for staying there."

"No, you shouldn't. He'd only be insulted if you did." He started to laugh. "Perhaps there's something to your vision book after all. Show me what else you've got in there. Oh, hang on. Didn't you say you were going to have some ice cream when you got home?"

"I did. I can get it later when I can walk again."

"I'll get it for you now. Which way to the kitchen?" He stood up.

"That door over there. Don't laugh at my small kitchen. It's nothing like yours. Can I have that ice cream with all the chocolate stuff in it, please? It's the first one that I made with you last night."

He shook his head. "I still don't know why you put so many different things in your creations. There was barely any room left for the actual ice cream." He looked down at his feet and seemed embarrassed. "I did come up with a name for it, though."

"Go on." Kira turned in her seat to get a better look at Ben's face. He looked cute when he was embarrassed.

Ben looked up and said, "Kira's Kaleidoscope."

"You've named it after me?" Kira was touched by his kindness.

He shrugged. "I have to name it something. I might sell it at my kiosk too. You can choose your favourite mix. I'll put a note to say you invented it. If that's alright with you?"

"Are you kidding me? An ice cream named after me? Of course that's alright!" She jumped in her seat. "Oo! My legs are starting to wake up."

"Don't make any sudden moves. Keep still until you've fully recovered. I'll be back in a minute with that weird ice cream you invented." He left the room.

"Hey!" she called after him. "That weird ice cream has got a name." She smiled to herself. It was nice having Ben here. She could be herself in his company. She looked again at the pictures of Edinburgh and a mad thought shot into her mind. Could she ask Ben to go with her to Edinburgh? They would have a great time together. She nodded to herself. Yes, she would ask him when he came back.

She flicked through the pages and listened as Ben moved around the kitchen. She stopped at a page which she'd filled with images years ago. Oh, she'd forgotten she'd put these photos in her book.

She was suddenly aware of Ben hovering behind her. He thrust a full bowl of ice cream at her and announced, "Seeing as your legs are better, I'll leave you alone. I'll see myself out."

Kira took the bowl and looked over her shoulder to see why Ben was suddenly so angry, but he had already left the room. She heard the front door slam as he left her home. Had she done something wrong? Was he disgusted by the state of her kitchen? It wasn't as fancy as his, but it was clean.

She frowned as she looked back at the images of her perfect man which covered two pages of her vision book. She didn't know what she'd done to upset Ben, but she'd sort it out as soon as she could. Of all the people in this town, the last person she wanted to fall out with was Ben.

Chapter 8

BEN

AT SEVEN MINUTES PAST eight the next morning, Ben pulled up the shutter of his kiosk to be met by the surly face of his first customer.

"You're late," Ted complained. "I've been waiting here for ages. What sort of a business are you running? An unreliable one, that's what I say. Leaving your customers waiting. It's not right."

Ben stared at Ted in silence. He was tempted to pull the shutter back down. Instead, he grunted, "What do you want, Ted?"

"An apology for a start." Ted raised his chin defiantly. "I'm going to be late for work because of you."

Ben glowered at Ted. "What do you want to eat?"

Ted hadn't finished complaining. He tapped his watch. "I should be heading into my office now. But no, I'm standing here waiting for you to open. Too much trouble, is it? Got better things to do, have you?"

Ben ran a hand across his forehead. He was already in a bad mood because of what he'd seen in Kira's vision book yesterday, and this stupid man was making his mood darken by the second. He really didn't need this hassle.

Ben abruptly declared, "Ted, you're barred."

Ted blanched. "Barred? What does that mean?"

"What do you think it means? You can't come to my kiosk anymore. And I won't serve you ice cream ever again. Is that clear?"

Sweat broke out on Ted's forehead. "You can't bar me. I've been coming here for years. I'm one of your most loyal customers."

"You don't sound like a loyal customer at the moment," Ben pointed out. "You sound like a moaning one. And I've got better things to do with my time than to listen to you moan. Go on, clear off." Ben made a move-away motion with his hands.

Ted's shoulders dropped, and he placed his hands on the counter. "Don't bar me, Ben. I need my ice cream. The thought of it was the only thing which got me out of bed this morning." He shook his head sorrowfully. "This diet the wife's put me on is worse than I thought. I didn't know there were so many varieties of lettuce, but my plate was piled high with the stuff last night. And the wife made me a vegetable smoothie for supper. Have you ever heard anything so disgusting? A vegetable smoothie!" He shuddered.

"That does sound vile," Ben agreed.

Ted continued, "That's not the worse of it. The wife had me doing exercises in the living room. She found this chap on YouTube who does this awful exercise programme. Throws himself all over the place, he does. It's not normal. The wife had a go at his warm-up and fell over the sofa. She's alright, by the way."

Ben frowned. "Why does everyone want to exercise all of a sudden?"

"Beats me. I walk to work and back every day, and that's enough for me. And do you know what, Ben?"

"What?"

"I like walking. I like looking at things as I walk along. I like saying hello to people too. You can't do that if you're whizzing past them at a hundred miles an hour."

"That's so true."

Ted gave him a small smile. "Sorry about complaining. It's the diet thing. I'm so hungry."

Ben nodded. "That's alright. What can I get you?"

"I'm not barred?"

"Not today, but watch your step." Ben tapped the board at the side of the kiosk. "Make a decision. Hurry up, I haven't got all day."

Ted's face lit up like a Christmas tree as he looked at the board of delights. His smile wavered. "Ben, what's this?"

Ben looked at where Ted has his attention. "You can read, can't you?"

"Yes, but it says frozen yoghurt. You don't sell frozen yoghurt."

"If it's on the board, then I sell it."

Ted blinked for a few seconds. "Is this a joke? If it is, I do not appreciate it, not in my weakened state."

"It's not a joke. I made some last night. What flavour do you want?"

Ted studied the board. His mouth twisted to one side as he looked at the frozen yoghurt flavours. He looked back at Ben. "I don't want yoghurt, I want the hard stuff. I'll have a large cornet with a scoop of triple chocolate ice cream, a scoop of strawberries and cream and some of that salted caramel sauce. Can you put some mini marshmallows and cookie crumbs on the top? Thanks. Oh, and stick two flakes in it."

"What about your diet? I don't want your wife coming down here and having a go at me."

"I don't care about that stupid diet. I like having ice cream, and no one is going to stop me eating it." He smiled broadly. "I gave myself a long look in the mirror this morning and thought, 'Ted, you're looking good, really good.' I'm happy with how I am, and no amount of lettuce will change that."

"Good for you," Ben said. "I wish everyone felt that way."

Ben busied himself with Ted's order. He smiled as he heard Ted whistling happily to himself. He preferred this version of Ted than the moaning one.

He handed Ted the huge ice cream and said, "Enjoy."

"Oh, I will." Ted paid for his treat. "Thanks, Ben. See you tomorrow." His loving attention remained on his ice cream as he walked away.

Ben watched him for a while. His thoughts went back to Kira. She was never far away in his thoughts. His heart twisted again at the images he'd seen in her vision book. There had been pictures of impossibly handsome men stuck on both pages. He'd seen the list of professions which the fantasy men had, and none of them included an ice cream vendor. Kira had also made a note of the names which her ideal man might have. There wasn't a 'Ben' listed amongst them.

He looked away from the beach. So, now he knew what Kira's ideal man looked like, where he worked and what his name was. And it wasn't him. At least he knew where he stood with her now. He'd been on the verge of asking her out yesterday, but seeing that vision book had made him change his mind. He wasn't sure how he was going to be with Kira when she turned up later. He'd do his best to be as friendly as always. The feelings he had for her were growing, and it was getting harder and harder to hide them. But that's what he had to do.

"Good morning, my dear Ben!" a man suddenly announced. "Isn't this a marvellous morning? Look at the colour of that sea. Have you ever seen it look so blue?"

"Morning, Reverend," Ben muttered. The last thing Ben needed was the ever-cheerful clergyman talking to him about the marvels of the day. He'd been hoping to wallow in self-pity for the rest of the morning, but that was impossible to do with Reverend Pendleton around.

Reverend Pendleton continued, "People are especially cheerful today, don't you think? So happy, and so generous with their smiles and good wishes."

"I hadn't noticed."

"And look at your lovely kiosk. So welcoming. Full of more treats than a person could eat in one month. This town is lucky to have you, Ben, so lucky."

Ben shrugged. "Do you want something to eat?"

"Not at the moment, thank you. I was out on my daily walk and thought I would call by and say hello to you. You're one of the town's most important residents. You do so much for this town with your delightful treats. We are truly blessed to have you here. And if ever I need your help, you never say no to me. No favour is too small for you. You always offer a helping hand." Reverend Pendleton beamed at him.

Ben's suspicions rose. "What do you want, Reverend?"

"Nothing." He continued to smile brighter than the lighthouse on a foggy night.

Ben's eyes narrowed. "You want me to do something for the church, don't you?"

"Well, now that you've brought the subject up, there is something you can help me with." He moved closer to Ben and placed his clasped hands on the counter. "The old folk at the retirement home are having a social event, and I could do with your assistance. You were a great help last time."

Ben sighed. "Is it another bingo night? I suppose I could do that, but tell Shirley Goodfellow to keep her hands to herself. I did not appreciate her sitting on my knee and stroking my hair."

Reverend Pendleton nodded. "I'll have a word with her. So, you'll do it then? This Wednesday at eight?"

"Eight in the morning? That's a bit early. I'll have to get someone to cover my shift here."

"No, eight at night. And it'll be in the church hall. See you then! Thank you, Ben. You are a shining star sent by the angels." He pulled his hands to his chest, gave Ben a kind smile and made to move away.

"Hang on there!" Ben called out. "There's something you're not telling me. Is the social event a bingo night? They usually have them at the retirement home."

"It's not a bingo night." The reverend took a step back. "It's a nineteen-sixties-themed dance. Thank you again." He took a step to the side like a crafty crab while still smiling at Ben.

"Get back here! I didn't know it was a dance. I don't do dancing."

"You'll love it. The old folk are so looking forward to it. You know what it's like at the retirement home, there are more women than men, so I need as many males as I can get." A twinkle came into his eyes. "It was Shirley Goodfellow who specifically asked for you. See you on Wednesday! Bring a friend if you like! Cheerio!" He shot off across the sand like a man forty years younger.

Ben shook his head at the departing man. He'd been hoodwinked. Again. That Reverend Pendleton was a sneaky one and no mistake.

Ben would go to the dance. He'd stay for thirty minutes, and that was all. And the next time Reverend Pendleton approached his kiosk, he would pull the shutter down and put the Closed sign out.

Ben checked the time. It would be a few more hours before Kira turned up. He would tell her about the dance and how Reverend Pendleton had tricked him.

Hope fluttered inside him for a second. Could he ask Kira to the dance?

No, of course not. She wouldn't want to waste her time on someone who wasn't her ideal man.

Ben's mood darkened once more. He looked at the customer who had just appeared. He barked, "What do you want?"

"Erm, I'm not sure," the woman said. "What have you got?"

Ben jabbed his finger at the board at his side and gave the woman a pointed look. It was going to be a long morning.

Chapter 9

KIRA

KIRA LET HERSELF INTO the library at the same time Ben was arguing with Ted. The library didn't open till nine on a Monday, but Kira wanted a bit of time to herself. Her thoughts were all over the place this morning, and they had been last night too.

It was Ben. She couldn't stop thinking about him. He'd always been a friend to her, but spending time with him in her home yesterday had changed that. He'd been such easy company, so very easy to talk to. And she hadn't forgotten how he'd rescued her from the park. He'd been like a hero in a van.

A smile came to her face as she pictured him carrying her across the threshold. It was quite a romantic thing to do, and he hadn't complained once about how heavy she was.

"Stop!" Kira said to herself. "No more of those thoughts. We agreed." She nodded to herself and headed to the kitchen. She put the kettle on and once again her thoughts returned to Ben. It was very annoying to be thinking about him so much, especially when she had stocktaking to do this morning.

She waited for the kettle to boil and wondered if things could go beyond friendship with Ben and her. Was that even a possibility? How did he feel about her? Was she just a loyal customer to him?

Kira rubbed her head in an effort to make sense of her thoughts. She tried to mentally file Ben away to the back of her mind. Life would be so much easier if she could control her thoughts that way; if she could file some thoughts and delete others. She would delete all self-deprecating thoughts from her mind if she could.

There was one thing she could get rid of straight away. She took her phone out and deleted her dating profile. Online dating wasn't for her. She couldn't be herself online. Well, maybe she could, but who would she attract then? Someone who loved ice cream as much as she did? Who loved the same books and films? Someone like Ben?

There he was again, popping into her head.

Kira made herself a strong cup of tea and went into the main area of the library. She made a list of all the jobs which needed doing that day. She liked this quiet time in the library. It was just her and the books. But that wasn't to say she didn't like it when people came in. There were some interesting people in this town, and Kira always enjoyed talking to them.

The time flew by with only a few more thoughts about Ben invading her mind. Kira made a fresh pot of tea for her colleagues who would be arriving soon.

As soon as the main library doors opened, Mrs Jenkins shuffled in. Her eyes widened in question as she made her way over to Kira behind the counter. The old woman asked, "Have you got it? Has it come in yet?"

"It certainly has. I've got it here." Kira reached under the counter and pulled out the latest release from Mrs Jenkins' favourite author. "Let me scan it for you."

Mrs Jenkins handed over her library card. "I can't wait to read this one! I know these books are a bit racy, but I do love them so. Takes me back to my youth. This latest one is based on a TV reality show. I read a sample on my computer last week. Oh my! You should read what those reality stars get up to in this book! Made me blush, it did."

Kira smiled. She'd had a quick peek inside the book earlier, and the first paragraph had caused her to close the book in red-hot embarrassment. She scanned the book and then gave it to Mrs Jenkins. "You enjoy it. Let me know if you want me to order anything else. Or you can order books online."

Mrs Jenkins hugged the book to her chest. "But I like coming in here and talking to you. You're like a friend to me. You never judge me by what I read, not like you-know-who." Her lips pursed in disgust.

Kira knew Mrs Jenkins was referring to her nosy neighbour who was forever poking her nose in Mrs Jenkins' business, according to the elderly woman anyway.

Worry crossed Mrs Jenkins' face and she shuffled closer to Kira. In a low, quiet voice, she asked, "Kira, is the library going to be okay?"

"What do you mean?"

"With all this stuff going on in town, you know. All the changes and improvements. I know that lass from London wants more tourists to come here, which I understand. But will they want a library? You don't go to a library when you're on holiday, do you?"

"I suppose you don't."

"What if that lass decides the library is no good to the town anymore? What if she wants to close it down?" Mrs Jenkins' chin wobbled. "I would hate that to happen. I love coming here. Lots of people do."

Kira said, "I don't think anything will happen to the library. Why don't I talk to Daisy Clarke and find out for certain? She's good friends with the mayor, and she might be able to ask Roberta about the future of the library."

"Would you? Will you let me know what she says?"

"Of course. Please, don't worry."

There was a polite cough behind Mrs Jenkins.

Kira looked that way to see Daisy Clarke standing there.

Mrs Jenkins blustered, "Oh, my dear, I didn't see you standing there. I hope you didn't think we were talking about you."

Daisy said kindly, "I did hear you talking about me, but I don't mind. I'd rather people tell me what's worrying them. It's Mrs Jenkins isn't it?"

Mrs Jenkins nodded.

Daisy continued, "I would never let anyone close this beautiful library. It's part of the town. If anyone should try, they'd have me to deal with. In fact, I was hoping to run some events here. I've spoken to Roberta, and she thinks it's just what the library needs." She looked over at Kira. "I wanted to talk to you about that. What can we do to get more people in here?"

Kira's glance went to Mrs Jenkins, and she said, "What about asking authors to come here? Is that something you could organise?"

"I could try. Have you got anyone in mind?"

Kira pointed to the book which Mrs Jenkins had a tight hold on. "How about that author? I know she's very famous, but is it a possibility?"

Mrs Jenkins paled slightly.

Daisy looked at the book, took her phone out and tapped on it. "I can certainly try. Let me see. Oh, great, she's got a website and a PR agent. I'll get in touch with her straight away."

Mrs Jenkins wavered on her feet. Daisy put her hand out to steady the woman. In a voice full of awe, Mrs Jenkins said, "Do you think she would come here? To our little town?"

"I'll do my best to persuade her," Daisy confirmed. "And if she does come here, I'll make sure you're on the front row when she gives a talk."

Tears filled the elderly woman's eyes. "You are an angel." She looked at Kira. "And so are you. Don't ever leave us, Kira. You're so reliable and dependable. This library wouldn't be the same without you."

Kira said goodbye to Mrs Jenkins and kept her eyes on the old woman as she left the library. Then she turned to Daisy and said, "Reliable and dependable? I'm not sure I want to be like that."

Daisy moved closer and gave her a long look. "Kira, what's wrong? You don't seem yourself today. Excuse me for saying so, but you look tired. Is something troubling you?"

"It's hard to explain. I feel restless, but I'm not sure why. I feel I should be making changes, but I don't know what those should be." She scrunched her face up. "Do you know what I mean? It's like someone has shaken me up, and now I can't get myself back together."

"Like a human kaleidoscope?"

Kira laughed at that. "That's the second time I've heard that word recently, but yes, like a kaleidoscope." The word brought Ben's face back to her. "Daisy, how did you know Jacob was the one for you? You seem like total opposites."

"We are. But there was something about him. He kept popping into my mind like an annoying bee. You know when you're sitting outside and trying to enjoy the sunshine and an annoying bee keeps bothering you? It was like that, only the bee was Jacob." Daisy laughed. "I'm not sure Jacob would like to be compared to a bee. Is there someone buzzing around your thoughts, Kira?"

"Perhaps." Kira sighed. "But I don't know what to do about it."

"When was the last time you had a holiday?"

Kira considered Daisy's question. "About six months ago. But before you say I should take a holiday, I can't. Holidays of over two weeks have to be booked months in advance here."

"How about taking a few days off?" Daisy suggested. "I've still got my apartment in London. You could stay there for a few days and sort yourself out."

"Oh, no, I couldn't do that."

"Why not?"

"Because—" Kira stopped talking. She couldn't think of one reason as to why she shouldn't take a few days off.

Daisy reached into her handbag and withdrew a set of keys. "Here, take these. The apartment isn't big, but it's got a great view. And there are loads of takeaway places nearby. You'll find menus pinned up on my noticeboard in the kitchen. Kira, it would do you good to get away for a while. You could make sense of your thoughts. Don't you think so?"

Kira took the keys, smiled at Daisy and said, "I do think so. Thanks so much, Daisy. I'll see if I can leave early today. No one will miss me if I take a few days off."

Daisy gave her a knowing look. "I wouldn't be too sure about that."

"What do you mean?"

"Nothing. I'd better get on. Help yourself to anything in the apartment. I'll text you the address in a few minutes. Bye for now. Phone me if you need anything."

Kira quickly headed into the staffroom to ask for time off. She had to do it quickly before she changed her mind.

Chapter 10

BEN

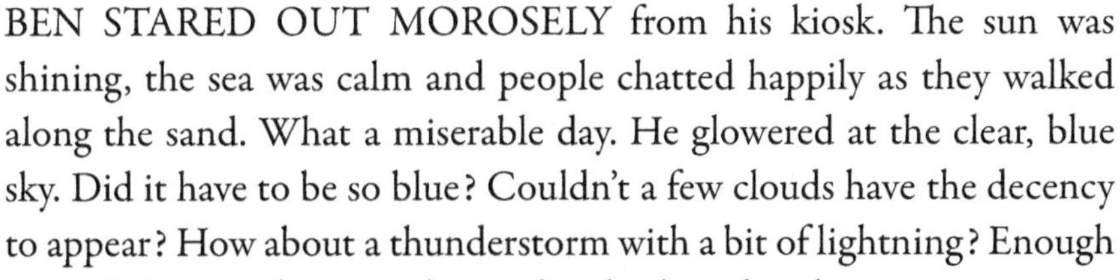

BEN STARED OUT MOROSELY from his kiosk. The sun was shining, the sea was calm and people chatted happily as they walked along the sand. What a miserable day. He glowered at the clear, blue sky. Did it have to be so blue? Couldn't a few clouds have the decency to appear? How about a thunderstorm with a bit of lightning? Enough to send those smiling people scuttling back to their homes.

Ben knew he shouldn't be taking his foul mood out on the weather or the innocent people in front of him, but he couldn't help it. Monday had been an awful day because Kira hadn't turned up to his kiosk. Ben had tried not to be too worried about her absence and reasoned she might be taking a day off from work and be out somewhere. But then Tuesday had come around, and Kira still hadn't shown up. And now here he was on Wednesday afternoon, and he still hadn't seen her.

"Your face could curdle a pint of milk," a cheery voice called out. "I hope you haven't been staring at your ice cream like that; it'll be ruined."

Ben scowled at Daisy. "What do you want?"

"A welcoming smile and a cheerful hello." She beamed at him. "That's not too much to ask for, is it?"

"I don't sell smiles and hellos; I sell ice cream. If you don't want anything, then leave me alone."

"My goodness, you are in a bad mood today." Daisy looked down at the grey-furred dog at her side. "Isn't he a miserable person today, Malcolm? Even worse than Jacob, and that's saying something."

Malcolm gave Ben a long look and then slowly nodded as if agreeing with Daisy's every word. Ben had known Malcolm for years and normally, the sight of the lovely dog cheered him up. But not today. Ben was too depressed to be cheered up by Malcolm's big eyes.

Ben said, "Is there something you want, Daisy? I'm busy."

"You don't look busy. What's wrong with you today?"

Malcolm sat down on the sand, tilted his head to one side and waited for Ben's answer.

Ben shrugged. "Nothing's wrong."

"Liar. I'm not going anywhere until you tell me what's wrong."

"Mind your own business and clear off!" Ben snapped.

"No, I won't. Anyway, we're customers." She reached into her pocket and pulled out some money. "I'll have a choc ice, please. And can Malcolm have some water? Thanks. We're going to stay here until you tell us what's wrong."

"Nothing's wrong. Stop being so nosy." Ben took her money. As angry as he was with Daisy, he wasn't going to turn business away.

"I'm not being nosy; I'm concerned." Daisy gave him a look full of concern to prove her point. "And Malcolm's concerned too."

Malcolm let out a little whine which almost made Ben smile.

Ben shoved a choc ice at Daisy along with her change. He said, "I'll bring Malcolm's water out."

"You really should have some tables and chairs out here," Daisy said. "You've got a great view here, and people would love to gaze at it while eating their ice creams."

"I don't want people hanging around my kiosk," Ben grumbled. He poured some water into the special dish he kept for Malcolm. He took it outside and placed it next to the dog. Malcolm leaned his big head against Ben's leg for a few seconds before turning his attention to the water. Ben appreciated Malcolm's comforting touch.

Daisy carefully tore her choc ice wrapper open. While keeping her eyes averted from Ben, she said, "You don't mind Kira hanging around your kiosk."

Ben's eyes narrowed, and he was about to tell the nosy woman to mind her own business again, but then he realised Daisy might know where Kira was. Even though Daisy had only lived in Holly Blue Bay a short while, she seemed to know everyone's business.

Ben knelt next to Malcolm and stroked his shaggy head. He said casually, "I haven't seen Kira for a few days. I think she's avoiding me." He added a light-hearted laugh to show he wasn't bothered at all by Kira's absence.

Daisy said, "She's in London. This is a delicious choc ice."

Ben straightened up. "London? What's she doing in London?"

"She needed some time to herself."

"Why? What's wrong with her?"

Daisy gave him a direct look. "She's a bit confused about her life, and she wanted some time to think about it."

"What's she confused about? She likes her life, doesn't she? She loves her job, and she's got lots of friends."

"Yes, but sometimes things happen which force you to think about your life. Things change around you, and you feel as if you want to change too. Don't you ever feel like that?"

"No." Ben folded his arms. "This is your fault, Daisy. Coming to our town with your fancy ideas! And now look what you've done."

Daisy pointed her choc ice at him. "Don't you shout at me, Ben Roberts. I'm doing an excellent job in this town. Many people have told me so."

Ben hadn't finished berating Daisy yet. "Why did Kira go to London then? Has that got something to do with you? Did you tell her to go there? To get as far away from me as possible? I've a good mind to take that choc ice back!"

Daisy squared up to him. "Just try it, mister." She kept her eyes firmly on him while taking a big bite of the choc ice.

Malcolm moved over to Ben and leaned his full weight against him. Feeling his warmth suddenly made Ben's anger drain away. He stroked Malcolm's head and said to Daisy, "Sorry. I know you're doing a good job. It's just that I—" He stopped talking and looked down at Malcolm.

Daisy said gently, "You miss Kira."

Ben nodded. "She's a good friend."

"She's more than a friend to you; any fool can see that." She smiled. "Except the fool who can't see it. Ben, you're a different person when Kira is around. You're almost human."

Ben gave her a half smile. "Steady on."

"It's true. I talked to Kira before she left for London, and I got the impression she's developing feelings for you."

"Oh? What sort of feelings?"

Daisy rolled her eyes. "Are you really so stupid? Romantic feelings, of course."

"Don't be daft. I'm not her ideal man."

"How do you know that?" Daisy shoved the last of the choc ice into her mouth.

"I saw pictures of her ideal man. She's got this vision-book thing, and there he was; her ideal man with his perfect job and his perfect name. Well, there was more than one man in her book but they all looked like models."

Daisy shook her head at him. "We all have ideas of who we think is perfect for us, but then someone comes along who's even better. Why don't you phone Kira and see how she's doing? I bet she'll love to hear from you. You have got her number haven't you?"

"Yes, but I can't phone her. What would I say? Anyway, if she wants some time alone then she doesn't want me bothering her."

Daisy gave him a shove which sent him backwards. She said, "You are so stubborn! And you're an idiot too. Of course Kira would want to hear from you! She's been gone for three days, and her closest friend hasn't been in touch. You could tell her how much you're missing her."

"She should have phoned me," Ben said in a sulking tone. He received another shove from Daisy. "Hey! Stop doing that!"

"Someone has to make you see sense. Phone her. Ask her how she is. Perhaps you could even ask her out on a date."

Ben scratched his head. "I can't do that."

"You can, can't he, Malcolm?"

Malcolm barked in response.

Ben shook his head. "But I don't know what to say to her." He threw his hands up in despair. "Oh, this is stupid! Kira doesn't think that way about me at all! Just because you're in a relationship with Jacob, you want everyone else to be in one too. You're too controlling, Daisy. Well, you can stop trying to control me. I won't have it." He jutted his chin out and moved towards his kiosk.

Daisy blocked his way. "What if I'm right, eh? What if Kira does like you but is scared to make a move, eh? What if you two never tell each other how you really feel? And on your deathbed, you'll clutch your chest where your shrivelled heart lives and you'll wail, "Daisy was right. I should have phoned Kira on that day many, many years ago. I should have listened to that wise woman. I am such a fool!" And then you'll die all alone." Daisy put her hand on her chest and let out a heartfelt sigh. "What a waste."

Ben said, "There's no need to be so dramatic. Shift out of the way. I've got work to do."

"There's every need to be so dramatic." Daisy beckoned Malcolm over and crouched at his side. "I need your help, dear friend. You take care of Ben for a bit. Impart your canine wisdom on him, okay?"

Malcolm nodded and then padded over to Ben's side.

Daisy continued, "Ben, take Malcolm for a walk and clear your head. Work out what you're going to say to Kira when you phone her."

"But my kiosk," Ben started to argue.

"I'll take care of that. I've been here enough times to know what goes on." Her eyes twinkled with mischief. "I'll try not to eat too much ice cream. Go on then; clear off."

"But I—"

"But nothing." Daisy put her hand on his arm. "Ben, you and Kira are meant to be together. You can't let this opportunity pass. You'll regret it forever if you do. And what if someone else came along and stole Kira's heart? How would that make you feel?"

Anger flashed through Ben. "I would not like that at all! Why are you saying that? Has someone been giving her the glad eye at the library?"

"I don't know what the glad eye is." Daisy turned away from him. "Have you got your phone with you?" She disappeared around the back of the kiosk.

"Yes."

Daisy appeared inside the kiosk. "Good, then use it. You've got a marvellous view from in here. And you're surrounded by ice cream. I'm going to enjoy being here." Her glance alighted on the board at her side. "Frozen yoghurt? What's that doing on your board? Are you selling it now?"

Ben answered quietly, "I made some for Kira."

Daisy held her arms wide. "You see, you're meant to be together. Look at what you do for her." She shooed him away. "Have a walk up to the lighthouse. You'll be in a better mood by the time you've reached it. Phone Kira from there. And when you come back, you can tell me what she said. Don't forget to tell her how much you've missed her."

Ben sighed. "I don't have a choice, do I?"

"No. And don't make Malcolm depressed! If you break Malcolm's spirit with your miserable mood, the whole town will be after you."

Malcolm wagged his tail as if to say his spirit would never be broken.

Ben walked away from his kiosk, Malcolm padded at his side. With every step he took, Ben's heart felt lighter and his bad mood melted away as if made of ice cream. He would phone Kira, and he would ask her out on a date.

He said to Malcolm, "She might even say yes. What do you think about that, Malcolm?"

Malcolm gave him a happy bark in reply which made Ben's spirits soar higher.

Chapter 11

KIRA

KIRA FELT HELPLESS tears filling her eyes. She blinked them away, this wasn't the time to cry. She had to phone him. He was the only one who could help her.

He answered on the first ring. "Kira! Hi. I was about to phone you."

She smiled at the warmth in his voice. "Ben, I need your—"

He interrupted her. "Daisy told me you'd gone to London. I didn't know where you were these past few days! I went round to your house last night to see if you had room in your freezer for that other tub of ice cream, but you weren't in!" He laughed. "Course you weren't in, you were in London. None of your neighbours knew where you were. I just called on a few of them to see if they knew where you'd gone."

"Ben, I've—" Kira tried again.

"Then I saw Daisy a bit ago, and she told me where you'd gone. London of all places!" He laughed again and Kira wondered for a second if he was drunk. He was never usually this chatty and cheerful. He carried on, "You'll never guess where I am. I'm on that bench up by the lighthouse, and Malcolm's here with me too. He's keeping me company."

Kira frowned. "Who's looking after the kiosk?"

"Daisy. I hope she doesn't eat all my choc ices. I should have counted them before I left her in charge. Not that it matters. It's good to hear your voice, Kira. I've been worried about you. When you didn't turn up to my kiosk as normal, I thought you might have gone off ice cream."

"Off ice cream? Are you crazy? Ben, have you been drinking?"

"No, I'm just happy to hear your voice. Kira, there's something I want to say to you." He let out a nervous laugh. "I'm not sure how to say it, but bear with me. Let me get the words in the right order."

"Ben," Kira said more insistently. "I need your help. My car's broken down on the way back to Holly Blue Bay and I can't fix it." There was a silence. "Ben? Are you still there? Did you hear me?"

His tone was less cheerful now. "You've broken down, and that's why you've phoned me?"

"Yes, I didn't know who else to phone." Kira hesitated. She had looked online for breakdown companies, but her instinct was to phone Ben. "I don't want to put you to any trouble, but you were the first one I thought of who could help me. Perhaps I should phone someone else after all."

"You thought of me first?" She heard a bark and assumed it was Malcolm, unless it was Ben making weird noises. Ben said, "Tell me where you are exactly and I'll get there as soon as I can."

Kira gave him the details and added, "I'm not on the main road. I've pulled into a lay-by with one of those mobile food caravans." She lowered her voice. "There are some strange people about. They keep giving me funny looks. A big, hairy man offered to help me, but I said no. I didn't like how he was looking at me." She stopped talking as a funny noise came over the phone. "Ben? What are you doing?"

"Running. Stay in your car and lock the doors. I'll be there in twenty minutes or less. Okay?"

"Okay. Thanks, Ben."

"It's okay," he gasped. "I don't think much of this running lark."

"You don't have to rush. I'll keep my doors locked." Kira averted her gaze from a line of truckers who were sitting outside the mobile café and watching her intently as if she were a TV programme.

Ben huffed a goodbye and then ended the call.

Kira gave the truckers a tight smile. They nodded and then turned their attention away from her. They weren't a threat at all. It was just her overactive imagination making her think the worst. It was all those real-life police documentaries she watched. And those horror movies where a woman broke down in the middle of nowhere, and then... She gulped. She hadn't broken down in the middle of nowhere, but that didn't stop her from feeling nervous.

She took her phone out and made a note to look for car maintenance classes. She didn't like feeling so useless when it came to cars. And there was no excuse to feel so useless. Perhaps old Toby at the town's garage could give her some of the basic information. Toby had been around cars for years and he knew everything about them. Whenever anyone had any problems with their vehicles, they would phone Toby. And he'd turn up with a smile on his face, knowledge in his eyes and a well-worn toolbox.

Kira smiled as she thought about Toby. Her thoughts wandered to the other residents of Holly Blue Bay. It was wonderful to live in a place where she knew so many people. London wasn't like that at all. London was an exciting place, and there was a lot going on, but it wasn't for Kira. She'd begun to miss her little town within an hour of arriving in London. And there was one person she'd missed more than anyone else.

Ten minutes later, the man who was occupying her thoughts turned up in his van. Her heart leapt for joy at the sight of him. Ben, her lovely Ben. She hadn't realised how important he was to her. Being away from him had made her miss him a lot.

Ben parked right in front of her car. Kira jumped out and ran over to him. Ben stepped out of his van and gave her that lovely smile of his. Kira was overcome with joy and threw herself into his arms. Loud cheers came from the nearby truckers.

"Hey, steady on," Ben said. "Are you okay? Has anyone been giving you any trouble?"

"No, not at all." Kira took a step back. "I'm pleased to see you. Thanks for coming here. You never let me down. I don't know what I'd do without you."

Ben gazed into her eyes. Kira swallowed. He'd never looked at her like that before. She liked it.

Ben said, "I never will let you down, Kira."

There were more cheers from the truckers and Kira blushed. She turned around and pointed to her car. "I don't know what's wrong with it. It was fine for a while, then it made a weird noise like it was coughing, and then the engine just died. I had a look under the bonnet, but I don't know what I'm looking for." She gave him an embarrassed smile. "I bet it's something really easy to fix. I should know how to fix my own car."

"Let's have a look together. I'll get my tools." Ben smiled at her again. "Did you have a good time in London?"

"It was okay. But I missed our town." She wanted desperately to say she'd missed him too, but the words wouldn't come out.

Ben surprised her by saying, "I missed you. Let's get your car sorted out and we'll get you back home." He went to his van and retrieved a toolbox.

Kira didn't move. She was basking in the warmth of his words. He'd missed her. Ben had missed her. But wait, had he missed her as a friend? Or as a customer? Or as something else?

Kira was brought out of her troublesome thoughts by Ben shoving something at her. It was a dirty cloth. He said, "We'll start with the basics. We'll check your oil and water first, and then the battery connections. Kira, don't take this an insult, but have you got enough petrol in?"

"I have. I filled up before I left London." She waved the cloth at him. "Show me what to do."

Ben opened the bonnet of her car and very patiently showed her how to check things inside. Kira stood close to him, not because she needed to, but because she wanted to. Being alone with her thoughts over the last few days had made her realise how much Ben meant to her. And as soon as she found her courage, she was going to tell him how she felt.

Ben soon identified the problem with her car, and together they fixed it. Kira's hands got covered in grime, but she didn't care.

Ben closed the bonnet and said, "I'll drive behind you on the way back to Holly Blue Bay. You shouldn't break down again, but if you do, I'll be right there."

Kira blinked. He was such a lovely man. Now would be the perfect time to tell him how she felt.

Ben's phoned beeped. "Sorry, let me get that. It might be Daisy. I gave her my number before I left. She was worried about you."

"She didn't need to worry. You were on your way to rescue me." She lifted her head and forced courage into herself. She would ask him out as soon as he'd finished his phone conversation. Where would they go on their date? Somewhere local? Perhaps she could cook for him.

Ben finished his call. "It was Daisy. I told her you were okay." He shook his head. "She's run out of choc ices. I think she's eaten them all herself. I'd better get back before she eats all my stock. Are you ready to go home?"

"Yes. But Ben, there's something I wanted to ask you." Kira's mouth felt dry and she couldn't continue. Crikey. What was going on? Why was her body letting her down? Come on, Kira, sort yourself out.

Ben said, "There's something I want to ask you too. Reverend Pendleton has roped me into another social event for the old folk. It's a sixties-themed thing and there'll be dancing. It's on tonight at the church hall. I'd love it if you would go with me."

"Me?" Kira blinked at him.

"Yes, you. If I have to dance, I'd rather dance with you than anyone else in the town."

"Dance?" Kira's mouth was letting her down badly and getting one word out was a struggle.

"Unless you don't want to?"

His smile was tender and Kira felt as she was floating inches off the ground. She managed to mutter, "Yes. I'd like that."

Ben clapped his hands together. "Great! Good! Super! Are you okay to drive home?"

Kira nodded, but she wasn't sure at all. Her limbs felt warm and floppy.

Ben grinned at her.

Kira grinned back.

The truckers cheered and someone yelled, "Kiss her!"

Ben said, "Let's get away from this rowdy lot." He got into his van and waited for her to get in her car.

Kira was still grinning as she got in her car and drove back to Holly Blue Bay. She had a date with Ben! She just knew something magical was going to happen tonight. She could feel it.

Chapter 12

BEN

LATER THAT EVENING, Ben checked his reflection in the rear-view mirror of his car. He smoothed his hair down and straightened his tie. He didn't look like any of those men in Kira's vision book, but he would have to do. His mouth was dry and his heart was beating far too fast. He hadn't felt this nervous in a long time. Why was he so nervous? He'd been friends with Kira for years, and they were only going to the church hall. But if he was honest with himself, Ben knew tonight was different. This could be the night their friendship changed into something else.

He smoothed his hair down again before getting out of his car. His legs felt wobbly as he walked towards Kira's door. Pull yourself together, man! He could hardly impress Kira if he collapsed in a jelly-like mess on her path. He straightened his tie once more as he stopped at her door. He raised his hand to knock and noticed how it was shaking slightly. He was in a bad way tonight, and it was all because of Kira.

Before he got the chance to knock, the door was flung open and a vision of beauty stood there.

"How do I look?" Kira twirled around. "I bought this dress years ago at a vintage shop. It's actually from the sixties. Look at how the skirt flies out when I twirl around." She spun again, a huge smile on her lovely face. She stopped and patted her hair. "What do you think

72

of this? Does it look like a proper beehive style? I've tried my best. I followed someone on YouTube. Does it look okay? And do I look presentable?"

Ben could only stare. He wanted to say that she looked amazing, stunning, beautiful and that she'd knocked the breath right out of his body. But words failed him, and only he could do was mutter, "You look fine."

Kira laughed. "I'll take that as a compliment." She put her hands on her hips and looked him over. "You do scrub up well. I've never seen you in a suit before. You look very handsome."

"Thanks," Ben muttered. He hoped he was going to do more than mutter tonight. "Are you ready to go?"

"Just a moment. I'll get my handbag." She turned away from him and headed down the hall.

Ben gave himself a mental shake. He was acting like an idiot. What was wrong with him? As Kira walked back to him, he knew what was wrong. He was in love with Kira, and he had to tell her that. He wasn't sure how he was going to do it, though.

Kira stepped out of the door and said, "Would you help me along the path, please? I'm not used to wearing such high heels. I got them at the same time as the dress. I must have known the perfect occasion would come up at some point, and now it has." She closed the door and locked it, and then reached for Ben's arm.

Ben's chest puffed out as he walked proudly down the path with Kira on his arm. It felt so right to have her there. He hoped all the neighbours were peeping out of their windows and having a good look at them.

He opened the passenger door for Kira and said, "In you go."

She gave him a regal nod. "Thank you, kind sir. I do hope you're going to serenade me on our journey."

"I'm not sure about that." He was finding it hard to put a sentence together, never mind a song. He smiled at Kira as she seated herself in the passenger seat. She smoothed her skirt down and placed her handbag on her knee. She smiled up at him which sent his pulse racing.

He walked around to the driver's side. He should have taken some of those herbal pills to calm himself down. One of his older customers swore by them, but Ben had always dismissed them as nonsense. But he could do with something to keep his nerves steady.

Once he was in the car, he put the radio on low, started the engine and said, "So, how did you get on in London? Did you have a good time?" He drove away from her house.

Kira asked, "Did Daisy tell you why I'd gone there?"

"She said something about you needing to sort your thoughts out."

"That's right."

"And did you sort your thoughts out?" Ben wasn't sure he wanted to know the answer.

"I did, and it didn't take me long to do so." He glanced over and saw her fiddling nervously with the strap of her handbag.

"Kira? Is there something you want to tell me? You're not thinking of making big changes in your life, are you? The sort that involves moving away?" He tried to laugh as if his heart wasn't breaking at that horrible thought. "You're not going to leave Holly Blue Bay and move to London, are you?"

To his relief, Kira laughed and said, "No, I like visiting London, but I don't want to live there. I did have time to think about my life, but do you know what, Ben?"

"What?"

"I came to the conclusion that I'm very happy with my life here. And I didn't know how wonderful it was until I started having a good think about it. I'm so grateful for everything I have."

Ben felt like he could punch the air in relief, but he kept his hands on the steering wheel. "That's good to hear. What are you happy about in particular?"

"My home, for a start. I love how cosy it is, and when I'm going to sleep, I can hear the sea in the distance. My neighbours are great, and will always take a package in for me if I'm not at home. I do the same for them if they're out. This is a silly thing, but Colin across the road always puts the bins away for those people who are at work all day. Isn't that a kind thing to do? He doesn't have to do it, but once the bins have been emptied, he puts them neatly away."

Ben nodded. "That's just how people are around here."

"I know, and that's why I'm so grateful. I thought about my job and realised how much I love it. I'm surrounded by books all day. And I love talking to the people who come in. It doesn't actually feel like a job when I'm at the library."

Ben smiled over at her. "So, you don't want to change your job?"

"Absolutely not! Oh, I haven't told you. Daisy's arranged for a famous author to visit the library. Mrs Jenkins will be over the moon when I tell her. Will you come to the event too? You could sell your ice cream there. I think people will need it after listening to that author read from one of her books."

"Oh? Why?"

"They're on the steamy side." Kira looked straight out of the window. "I don't read them."

Ben smiled as he saw Kira blush.

Kira fiddled with her handbag again.

Ben asked, "You seem nervous. Is there something else you want to tell me?"

She cast him a small smile. "There is. But can we talk about it later? We're almost at the church hall."

"Is it something I need to worry about?" Ben pulled into the church car park.

"No. At least, I hope not. It's something else I realised when I was away." Kira's eyes widened. "Ben, look at all the minibuses in the car park. They're not all from the town's retirement home."

Ben looked at the line of minibuses. "They've come from all over going by the names on the sides. This is a bigger event than I thought. Reverend Pendleton never told me it was going to be this big." He shook his head. "But that doesn't surprise me."

"It's good news, though," Kira said. "It's getting more people to our town."

Ben sighed and switched the engine off. "It's not good news for me. There's going to be a lot of elderly women in there without a dancing partner. I could be in demand."

Kira put her hand on his arm. "I'll make sure I rescue you now and again."

Ben looked into her eyes. "Promise?"

"I promise. And if I'm not successful, can you save a dance for me?"

"You can have all my dances."

Kira smiled. "I don't think Reverend Pendleton will allow that. He's standing at the door and waving frantically at you."

Ben's shoulders dropped. "I feel like I'm going into battle. We don't have to stay long. Perhaps ten minutes will be enough."

"You know you'll never get out in ten minutes." She patted his arm. "You can do this. Be strong."

"As long as I dance with you at some point, then I can get through anything. Would you like help getting across the car park?"

Kira nodded. "Yes, please."

Ben felt pride burst through him again as he escorted Kira across the car park. Reverend Pendleton was jumping up and down with impatience at the church hall door, but Ben ignored him. He decided there and then he would tell Kira he loved her tonight.

Chapter 13

KIRA

KIRA KEPT STEALING glances at Ben as they walked across the church car park. He looked so handsome tonight. She held on to his arm proudly and thought about the conversation she wanted to have with him. The butterflies in her stomach did a nervous dance at that thought.

Reverend Pendleton was hopping from foot to foot as they approached him. He exclaimed, "Ben! You're here at last. I'm going to have a riot on my hands if you don't get inside and start dancing. Come on! Come on!"

Ben said, "Not so fast. I'm helping Kira into the hall. She's having a bit of trouble walking in her heels." He smiled at her and she could see the care in his eyes. It was nice to be smiled at like that. And it took her mind off the lie she'd told him about her shoes. She could walk perfectly well in them on her own, but she wanted to be close to him. She was such a cheeky minx sometimes.

Reverend Pendleton pulled at his dog collar. "I didn't think so many people would turn up. The hall is packed with grey-haired pensioners. Daisy's done a good job getting the word out about this evening. In fact, she's done too much of a good job. I hope we've got enough food and drink."

Kira suggested, "Ben and I can always nip out for some more if needed. Can't we, Ben? We can go together."

"We certainly can."

Kira looked at the ground. That sneaky minx side of her was out in full force tonight.

Ben led her into the hall with Reverend Pendleton close behind.

They stopped just inside the hall and took in the view.

Wow!" Kira exclaimed. "This looks amazing. Look at all the twinkling lights in the ceiling! And the bunting! And the glitter! It looks so magical. What do you think, Ben?"

Ben was looking at her and didn't seem to be taking the surroundings in at all. He said softly, "Everything is beautiful, just beautiful."

Reverend Pendleton suddenly yelled, "Incoming!"

Ben was abruptly whipped away from Kira by an old woman in a long, red dress. The old woman had a determined look in her wrinkle-lined eyes. Kira caught a glimpse of Ben's terrified face as he was whisked away, and then he was lost in the throng of grooving pensioners on the dance floor.

Reverend Pendleton shook his head sadly and announced, "And that was the last time they saw Ben Roberts. His memory lives on."

"Who was that?" Kira asked.

"Shirley Goodfellow. She likes Ben, she likes him a lot. I did have a word with her earlier and told her not to scare the poor boy away. But alas, it seems my words fell on deaf ears. Which is a possibility because most people here forget to turn their hearing aids on when I talk to them. On purpose, I might add."

"I hope he's okay. Should I rescue him? He did promise to dance with me later."

The reverend gave her a look which she couldn't work out. He said, "If he's promised to dance with you, Kira, then that's what he'll do." There was a sudden commotion at the other end of the dance floor.

"Looks like some of the older gents have resorted to fisticuffs. That's what happens when I put too much rum in the rum punch. I should have known better than to allow alcohol in here tonight. Excuse me while I go and glower at them. I find a furious glower from me can work wonders. Enjoy the evening, my dear Kira. And before I forget, let me say how beautiful you look tonight. And furthermore, you and Ben make a lovely couple."

"But we're not a couple!" Kira called out as the reverend dashed away.

"Who's not a couple?" Daisy appeared at her side.

Kira jumped. "You scared the life out of me then." She grinned. "You look great. We've got similar dresses on."

"I thought I should make an effort. I like your hair. I tried to do that with mine but it looked more like a bird's nest than a beehive, so I gave it up as a bad job." Daisy glanced around the dance floor. "Are you here with Ben?"

"I am. He picked me up a bit ago. It was him who invited me here."

Daisy turned enquiring eyes on Kira. "Did he now? That's interesting. I hope he's showered you with compliments and told you how beautiful you look."

Kira shrugged. "Sort of. He looks very handsome tonight; don't you think so?"

Daisy scanned the room. "Where is he?"

Kira pointed. "There. He's being flung around by that woman in the red dress."

"Crikey! I doubt he'll make it out of here alive. I know we're short on men, but I don't want to lose one of them so early in the night."

"Should I go and rescue him?" Kira poised herself to move forward. "I think he needs rescuing, don't you? And I should do it. Don't you think so?"

Daisy placed one hand on her hip and gave Kira a long look. "You love Ben. I can see it in your eyes. Well, I've seen it for days."

"I don't love him!" Kira declared hotly. Her shoulders dropped. "That is such a lie. I do love him. As soon as I left town on Monday, I began to miss him terribly. I couldn't stop thinking about him while I was in London. You don't realise how important someone is until you're away from them. I'm going to tell him tonight. He promised to dance with me later." She put her hand on her stomach. "I'm so nervous!"

Daisy flapped a hand at her. "You'll be fine."

"I don't know about that. What if he's repulsed by me?"

"Pah! As if!"

A third person joined them. It was Jacob, the local handyman and Daisy's boyfriend. He was wearing a suit and looking uncomfortable.

He said to Daisy, "Who are you talking about? I don't know why I have to wear this suit and tie. I feel like I'm being strangled."

Daisy said, "You look dapper in that suit, so stop moaning. We were talking about Ben. I was laughing at the thought of him being repulsed by the beautiful Kira here."

Jacob frowned. "Why would he be repulsed? He loves her. Everyone in town knows that. That's the only reason he works at the kiosk; it's so he can see Kira every day."

Kira froze. Jacob snapped his mouth shut. Daisy folded her arms and glowered at Jacob.

Kira said, "I didn't know that. About Ben loving me or the kiosk thing. Why didn't anyone tell me?"

Jacob held his hands out in defence. "I thought you knew. Even I know, and I can be really dumb about these things. Just ask Daisy."

"But I don't understand," Kira said to Jacob. "Why didn't Ben say something to me?"

Jacob let out a nervous laugh. "I've no idea. I've said too much already. Have you seen Malcolm? I brought him in with me. Where is that dog?" He scooted away from them in a flash.

Kira was full of questions. "Daisy, did you know about Ben and how he felt?"

"Seeing as he growls and shouts at everyone except you, then yes, I did know how he felt." Daisy put her arm around Kira's shoulders. "I'm sorry you had to find out this way. I suspect Ben has been wanting to tell you for a long time. He was devastated when you left town. He said he was going to phone you and tell you how much he missed you. Did he tell you?"

"No." Kira thought back to the earlier phone call. "It was me who phoned him when I asked him to rescue me. But he was very chatty on the phone, which wasn't like him. Maybe he was trying to tell me something then, but I never gave him the chance."

Daisy squeezed her shoulders. "Perhaps he's going to tell you tonight when you're having a slow dance. But for the sake of my nerves, will one of you say something!"

Kira smiled as she looked over at Ben. He raised his hand in greeting and her heart filled with love. She said to Daisy, "Before this night is through, Ben will know how I feel."

Daisy took her arm away. "He's coming this way. This could be your chance."

Kira braced herself and gathered all the courage she could.

Ben wasn't alone when he came over. He had a small, fragile-looking woman holding on to his arm. They stopped in front of Kira and Daisy, and Ben said, "This is Estelle. The amazing woman who owned the ice cream kiosk before me."

"Oh, yes!" Kira smiled at the woman. "Ben told me about that huge ice cream you made for him. He made the same one for me a few days ago."

Ben laughed. "I tried, but I don't think I captured the magic of the one you made me, Estelle."

Daisy looked bewildered so Kira explained. "Ben came here with his family when he was young. They bought ice creams from Estelle's kiosk. Ben's brother dropped his, so Ben gave him his ice cream. Estelle saw this and gave Ben a huge ice cream with everything on it. And I mean everything!"

Daisy grinned. "I like the sound of that. I bet you enjoyed that, Ben."

Ben looked at his feet. "Yeah, I did."

Estelle gave him a nudge in the ribs and said sharply, "Ben? Didn't you tell your lovely friend here the end of that story?"

Ben was still looking at his feet. "There's not much to tell."

Estelle let out a loud tut and shook her head at him. She looked at Kira and said, "Ben didn't get the chance to eat that ice cream because his foolish brother dropped his second ice cream. I was watching the little fella, and I saw exactly what happened. Ben's brother took one look at the big ice cream I'd given to Ben, and he threw his half-eaten one on the sand on purpose! The cheeky pup!"

"He didn't!" Kira exclaimed.

"Oh, he did. And then this charming man at my side handed over that ice cream I'd made just for him."

Ben finally looked up. He shrugged and gave Kira a small smile. "He's my brother. What else could I do?"

Kira's heart seemed too large for her chest as it swelled with more love for this generous, caring, thoughtful, handsome man in front of her. Her voice was thick with emotion as she said, "Ben, we need to dance right now. I have to tell you something, and it can't wait a minute longer."

Chapter 14

BEN

BEN TOOK KIRA GENTLY by the elbow and led her onto the dance floor. Even though he'd been flung around the church hall by energetic pensioners, he'd kept looking over at Kira. He had found it impossible to keep his eyes off her; she looked amazing and even more beautiful than ever.

They stopped in the middle of the floor and Ben asked, "Are you having a good time?"

"I am now." She put her arms around his neck. "I need to tell you something."

"I need to tell you something too." Ben forced himself to stay calm even though his heart was beating like crazy. Was this the best time and place to tell Kira he loved her? He smiled at her. Any time and place were perfect.

"Let me go first," Kira said.

"No, let me. If I don't say it now, I fear my nerves will get the better of me." He swallowed nervously.

An elderly woman abruptly appeared at his side and snaked a bangle-covered arm around his waist. "Ben, you said you'd dance with me. Come on, you can dance with your young lady later." She cackled. "I might be dead tomorrow! I have to make the most of the time I've got left." She attempted to pull him away.

Ben said, "Linda, you're going to outlive all of us. I will dance with you later, but right now, I'm dancing with Kira."

Linda tugged on his arm some more. "Kira doesn't mind, do you?" She aimed a bright smile at Kira.

To Ben's immense relief, Kira said firmly, "I do mind, actually. I've got something important to tell Ben, and it won't wait." A kind look came into her eyes. "As soon as I've finished with him, I'll bring him over to you."

Linda looked at Ben, and then back at Kira. She relented, "Okay, but don't be too long. I've been waiting a while to get my hands on this young man." She treated Ben to a cheeky wink before sauntering away.

Kira laughed. "You are in demand tonight."

"I don't want to be." He gave his full attention to Kira. "You look wonderful tonight." He cleared his throat. "You look wonderful all the time. I missed you when you were away."

Kira gave him a shy smile. "I missed you too. Jacob just told me something about the kiosk, but I don't know if he was joking. Ben, why do you work at the kiosk? You've got employees who could do that for you."

He put his arms around her waist and swayed to the gentle music. "I used to have staff there, but one day, they were all off sick at the same time. So, I had to run the kiosk. Later that day, an amazing woman turned up and asked for a tub of mint choc chip. She had a lovely smile which lit up the day. And when I gave her the ice cream, she smiled even more and her eyes were alive with joy, all at the sight of that ice cream."

Kira blushed. "Are you talking about me? It was excellent ice cream."

Ben pulled her a fraction closer. "You stayed to talk to me, and you asked about my day. Most of my customers clear off once they've got their ice creams, but you didn't. It's like you had all the time in the world to chat with me."

Kira shrugged one shoulder. "You intrigued me. I thought anyone who made such delicious ice cream must be an amazing person. I wanted to know more about you."

"I'm glad you did. We've become good friends over the years. You're part of my life. When you went away, I felt like my heart was broken. I was worried you weren't going to come back." He faltered as fresh memories of Kira's absence tugged at his heart painfully.

Kira said, "I thought about you all the time when I was in London. Don't be insulted, but I bought some ice cream from a vendor on the street."

Ben let out a mock gasp of outrage. "I feel so betrayed."

Kira laughed. "You don't need to. It was awful. I had to throw it away, that's how bad it was."

The music sped up, but Ben and Kira didn't. They continued to sway gently together.

"Kira, I have to say this. I—"

He was roughly pulled out of Kira's arms. For a second he thought it was an impatient Linda, but it wasn't.

Reverend Pendleton's words came out in a rush. "Oh Ben! So sorry for interrupting you, but there's been an accident! Shirley Goodfellow has hurt herself doing the twist! I was there when it happened. I heard something crack!"

Ben spun around and saw a group of people looking down at someone on the floor. The music came to a sudden stop and he heard the moans of a woman in distress.

Reverend Pendleton continued, "We can phone for an ambulance, but it'll be quicker if you take her to the hospital. You can use one of the smaller minibuses and lay her across the back seat."

Ben ran a hand across the back of his neck. "I don't know about that. We shouldn't move her."

There was another moan and then Shirley's voice called out, "Linda, stop making that dreadful noise! I'm not dead. Not yet. Move out of the way and let me get up."

The crowd parted and a dishevelled Shirley got to her feet.

"She's alive! It's a miracle!" Reverend Pendleton moved towards Shirley. Ben and Kira went after him.

Shirley was patting her hair and complaining. "I only slipped. There's no need to make such a fuss. Who turned the music off? Oi, you behind the turntable, put the music back on. I came here to dance."

The reverend stopped in front of Shirley, concern on his face. "My dear woman, are you sure you're okay? You went down with some force. And I heard something crack. Was it your hip?"

Shirley patted her hips. "No, I'm fine. Still in one piece." She grimaced and pulled something from her dress pocket. She let out a couple of curse words and said, "My flask! I only bought it last week. The gin's leaked out. What a waste."

Ben shared a look with Kira. Kira's mouth twitched as she tried not to smile.

Reverend Pendleton took the dripping flask from Shirley and said, "I'll get rid of this for you. You didn't need to bring gin with you. I have provided alcohol."

"Yeah, but not much, and you've only got the weak stuff." Shirley took a step forward and winced. "I'm ready to dance again. You can all stop gawping at me. I slipped, that's all."

"Did your slip have something to do with your gin consumption?" the reverend asked innocently.

"Reverend, this is no place for a sermon." She took another step, grimaced and the colour drained from her face.

Ben caught the elderly woman as she slowly fainted. She weighed barely anything. Ben said, "I'm taking her to the hospital. She might have banged her head."

Kira said, "I'll come with you."

"No," Reverend Pendleton interjected. "I'll go with Ben. It's my fault she's hurt herself. I should have frisked her for hidden booze when she came in. It's not the first time she's done this. Kira, would you be an absolute dear and keep an eye on events here, please? You're so efficient and organised; I know I can rely on you. Daisy is in charge of the event, but I know she'll need help when it comes to getting the old folk out of the hall and onto their buses." He glanced at the silent Shirley. "Hopefully, we won't be too long."

Kira looked torn and gave Ben a hopeless look. He said to her, "We can continue our conversation later."

She nodded. "Of course. Reverend Pendleton, I'll take care of things here. Have you got a list of everyone and which buses they should go on? I don't want anyone going home on the wrong bus."

"Daisy's got all the information. Bless you, Kira, you're already taking charge. You are a wonderful person to have in a crisis. Ben, isn't Kira wonderful?"

"She certainly is." Ben gave Kira a smile full of love before he turned away and left the church hall.

With the reverend's help, Ben placed Shirley on the back seat of his car. She was starting to come around and kept mumbling about gin.

Luckily, they were seen to straight away at the hospital. After examining her, the doctor concluded Shirley had a mild concussion and should be kept overnight for observation. Ben knew Shirley was back to her normal self by the cheeky smiles and winks she kept giving him.

As she was tucked into bed by a nurse, she said, "Ben, I think you should stay right by my side all night. I might have a funny turn and need the arms of a young, strong man around me."

Reverend Pendleton offered, "I'll stay with you."

Shirley pursed her lips at his words. "I don't want you. I want Ben to stay with me. He can hold my hand." She waved her hand at the armchair next to the bed. "Sit there, Ben, where I can reach you."

Ben cast a helpless glance at the door. "Shouldn't the doctor give you some sleeping pills or something?"

Shirley batted her eyelashes at him. "You can hold me in your arms and sing sweet lullabies until I nod off."

Reverend Pendleton produced a small black book from his pocket. "I can do better than that. I'll read you some of my favourite passages from the Bible." He turned to Ben. "You get back to the church hall. You don't want to keep your young lady waiting. Thank you so much for helping me tonight. You've gone well beyond the call of duty!"

Ben didn't need telling twice. He left the hospital as quickly as he could and drove back to the church hall. There was still time to dance with Kira, and plenty of time to tell her he loved her.

Ben arrived at the church hall, jumped out of his car and raced into the building where the festivities were still underway. He stood at the entrance and searched for Kira's lovely face. Ah! There she was. Ben rushed over to her.

Kira wasn't alone. She was talking to a handsome man and laughing. The words she said to the man brought Ben's world crashing down.

He spun around and raced out of the hall, his heart full of pain.

Chapter 15

KIRA

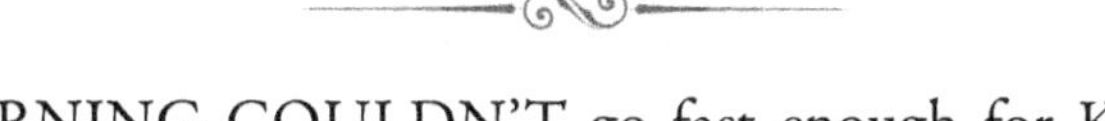

THE MORNING COULDN'T go fast enough for Kira. She was desperate for lunchtime to come around so she could leave the library and go to Ben's kiosk.

She recalled how the previous evening had ended. It still didn't make any sense to her. She had mingled with the pensioners while she'd waited for Ben to return to the church hall. It was while she was talking to Mrs Jenkins and her nephew that Kira had spotted Ben coming into the hall. She'd tried to tie-up the conversation she was having so she could give Ben her full attention. But when she'd looked Ben's way again, she saw him running out of the hall as if the building were on fire.

Kira had waited for Ben to return, but he never did. She had checked the car park and found his car had gone. Even though she'd phoned him several times to make sure he was okay, he hadn't answered. She'd tried him again this morning but he still hadn't answered his phone.

She checked her watch for the hundredth time and let out a sigh of irritation. Why was the morning dragging so much?

Maureen tapped her on the shoulder and said, "I don't know what's bothering you this morning, but you're really getting on my nerves with your constant time-watching."

"Sorry, I'm waiting for lunch to come around." Kira pointed to her watch. "Is this the right time? I think my watch has broken. It's going too slow. What time do you make it?"

"The same as you. Kira, do me a favour and go for an early lunch."

"I can't go now. It's far too early."

Maureen put her hands on Kira's shoulders, turned her around and aimed her at the doors. "Don't take this the wrong way, but get out and don't come back until you've done whatever needs doing so urgently." She gave Kira a push.

Kira gave her a grateful smile, grabbed her handbag from under the counter and scuttled out of the doors before Maureen could change her mind.

Kira headed to Ben's kiosk and almost broke into a run at one point. Was Ben okay? Had he been taken ill last night?

She stopped at the kiosk with a smile ready on her face. A young man stared out at her and asked, "Morning. What can I get you?"

Kira frowned. "You're not Ben."

"No, I'm not. What would you like?"

Kira leaned on the counter and peered into the kiosk. "Where's Ben? Why isn't he here? Is he poorly?"

"He looked alright when I saw him earlier," the man answered. "Could you step back a bit, please? You nearly knocked the chocolate flakes over then."

"But where is he?" Kira continued to peer into the kiosk as if expecting Ben to be hiding in a corner.

"I don't know. I think he's at the factory or in his office. Whoa! Watch the flakes!" The man whipped the box of chocolate flakes away from Kira. "If you don't want anything, can you move out of the way?"

Kira stood back and looked up and down the beach. Where was Ben? Something wasn't right. Ben was always in his kiosk. Why wasn't he here now?

Kira left the beach, got into her car and headed to the farm where Ben lived. She knocked on the door of the huge ice cream barn. A woman in a white hat and overalls answered it and informed her Ben was in his home.

"Is he poorly?" Kira asked.

The woman shook her head. "No, but I think he's got company." She closed the door before Kira could ask her any more questions.

Kira pressed her lips together grimly as she headed to Ben's cottage at the rear of the barn. She'd been all set to tell Ben she loved him last night, but that hadn't happened. She still wanted to tell him, but that wasn't going to be possible until she actually found him.

As Kira rounded the corner, she came to a sudden stop. Ben was standing at the door of his cottage. He was talking to a slim, blonde woman who was laughing loudly. The woman was holding a tub of ice cream.

Kira flattened herself against the wall of the barn and tilted her head so she could hear what Ben and his companion were saying. It didn't bother her at all that she was eavesdropping.

Ben said, "I hope you enjoy that. Make sure you get it into a freezer as soon as possible."

"I'm sure I will," the mystery woman replied with a laugh. "I've never made my own ice cream before! And in such an amazing kitchen too."

Kira stiffened and her blood ran cold. That woman had been in Ben's kitchen? And she'd made some ice cream there?

Ben laughed and said, "Anytime. It was a pleasure meeting you."

"Same here. I'll be in touch about seeing you next week. I'm warning you now that I'll be going back into your kitchen. This tub won't last me long at all."

Anger rushed through Kira. Who was this woman? And how dare she make ice cream with Ben! If anyone was going to make ice cream in Ben's kitchen, it should be her. Kira shifted position and stole a look at the woman. Her heart dropped like a stone when she saw the woman kiss Ben on the cheek.

Tears sprang to Kira's eyes and she turned away from the happy couple. Ben wasn't interested in her; he never had been. And why would he be? Kira was small and plump, she wasn't anything like the vision of loveliness who was standing in front of him with her freshly made ice cream. Her ice cream was probably perfect too, and not the messy concoction which Kira had made.

She took a heavy step away from Ben's home. Jacob had been wrong about Ben being in love with her. Ben didn't consider Kira anything other than a friend, it was clear now.

Kira's steps sped up. She wanted to get away from here as quickly as possible. She raced over to her car and fumbled in her pocket to find her keys. She'd nearly made a complete fool of herself last night at the church hall. Imagine if she had told Ben she loved him! He would have been mortified.

Kira's vision blurred as tears filled her eyes. As she blinked them away, something blue flashed in front of her. It was a butterfly. It landed briefly on Kira's car, and then just as swiftly, it flew away.

Something about its movements caused Kira to stop and stare into the distance. She couldn't leave yet. She had to do something. She had to be true to herself.

Kira spun around and marched back to Ben's cottage. He was still standing at the door talking to the blonde woman. Kira marched right up to them.

Kira jabbed her finger at Ben and yelled, "You! Ben Roberts! I want a word with you."

Ben jumped at the loudness of her voice. "Kira? What's wrong?"

"What's wrong?" Kira put her hands on her hips. "What's wrong, eh?"

Ben gave her a confused look. "Do you want to go inside?"

"No I do not!" Kira replied. She knew how loud her voice was but she couldn't seem to control it now.

The blonde woman spoke, "Perhaps I should leave you two alone."

"Don't leave on my account," Kira snapped. "I won't be long. I'll say what I've got to say and then I'll be off."

Ben's brow wrinkled. "Kira, why are you shouting?"

"Because I want you to hear me!" Kira took a step closer. "I want you and the whole town to hear me!"

"I think the next three towns over can hear you. Kira, come inside." Ben made a move towards his front door.

"Don't move!" Kira ordered. "Ben Roberts, I love you! Did you hear that? I love you! I was going to tell you last night when we were dancing, but pensioners kept getting in the way."

Ben's eyes widened. "What did you just say?"

"That pensioners kept getting in the way."

Ben shook his head. "Not that bit, the other bit. Did you say you love me?"

"Yes! And I'll say it again." Kira threw her head back and yelled, "I love you, Ben Roberts!" She looked back at him. "I know you don't love me, but I had to tell you. I can't be a caterpillar all my life. I'm a butterfly, and this is how I look. On the short side, and on the plump side. But this is me. I'm not changing for anyone. I love you, and I had to let you know." She gave him a firm nod.

Ben's face creased up as he smiled at her. "I love you too."

"Pardon?" Kira asked. His words took the wind right out of her angry sails. "Say that again."

Ben threw his head back and yelled, "I love you, Kira Dawson!" He looked back at her. "And I don't want you to change any part of yourself. You're perfect as you are."

Kira stared at him. Then she looked at the blonde woman who was smiling broadly. Kira asked her, "Did he just say he loved me?"

The woman nodded. "He did. You must be Kira."

Kira blinked. This situation was getting weirder by the second.

The woman explained, "I'm Tilly, Daisy's friend. She told me about you and Ben, and how it's taking you forever to get together. I came here to talk to Ben about setting up a website for his ice cream business."

Ben added, "It was Daisy's idea. That woman never gives up."

Tilly wagged her finger at him. "I don't give up either. I'll phone you next week about getting you online. I'll leave you two lovebirds alone. Bye for now!" She smiled before walking away.

Kira raised her hand feebly at Tilly. "I thought you and her—" Her hand dropped.

"Me and Tilly? Why? I only met her this morning."

"But she's been in your kitchen. And she's made ice cream."

Ben smiled. "It's all for the website. She's taken lots of photos. I thought it was time to get a website, and it'll shut Daisy up too." His smile dropped. "Anyway, you're a fine one to talk. You met your perfect man last night. I saw you at the church hall."

Kira frowned. "What? Who? When?"

"When I came back from the hospital. I saw you talking to that tall fella with dark hair. I heard you tell him he sounded like your perfect man. He looks like one of those men in your vision book too."

Kira put a hand over her mouth to stifle a laugh. "Oh, Ben, he works in a chocolate factory. That's why I said he sounded like my perfect man." She lowered her hands. "I'm sorry if that upset you. Is that why you left? And why you haven't been taking my calls?"

Ben gave her a small nod.

Kira sighed, shook her head and moved closer to him. "We are a couple of fools, aren't we?" She put her arms around his neck. "But this fool loves you."

Ben placed his arms around her waist and pulled her closer. "This fool loves you back."

Then they kissed.

Kira's body flooded with warmth and love.

Fireworks exploded in Kira's head as the kiss deepened — a kaleidoscope of fireworks.

Epilogue

Fourteen Months Later
KIRA

"CAN'T YOU GIVE ME A clue?" Kira asked Ben as they walked hand in hand along the beach. "Just a tiny clue? Go on."

"No chance. Be patient." Ben lifted the parcel. "You can open it when we get to the bench next to the lighthouse."

"But it's so far away." Kira let out a dramatic sigh. "And we've been walking for ages now."

Ben smiled at her. "We've been walking for exactly ten minutes. I thought you liked strolling along the beach with me."

"I do, but you've never had a mysterious parcel in your hand before." Kira's eyes narrowed as she glanced at the paper-covered package. "Is it ice cream? A new flavour? If it is ice cream, you should let me have it now before it melts."

Ben's smile increased. "It's not ice cream. Forget about the package for a while and enjoy this lovely evening. Look how blue the sea is."

"It's always blue. Is it a box of chocolates? Let me open it; we don't want the chocolates going off."

Ben swung Kira's hand back and forth. "I'm going to ignore your persistent questions. Let's talk about something else. Tell me more about the literary event you're doing at the library."

The thought of the event brought a smile to Kira's face. "Oh, Ben! It's going to be huge. We won't be able to fit in all the events at the library; some will take place at the town hall. Daisy's been so busy organising everything. She thinks we could do a beach party for the children to end the event. She's got some really famous authors coming."

Ben nodded. "It's not all down to Daisy. I know how hard you've worked too."

"I'm having a great time organising it all. I never imagined such famous people would come to our town." She nodded at the package. "Have you got me a book? Is that what it is? I hope it's another travel book. I can never get enough of those. Is it something for our next holiday?"

"It's not a travel book." Ben aimed a cheerful greeting at an elderly couple who passed them. They gave him uncertain smiles in return. Ben chuckled. "People are always surprised when I smile at them. I must have been a miserable bear of a man before."

"If you were, I never noticed."

They headed along the coastal path and towards the lighthouse.

Ben said, "I can't believe how much my life has changed since you declared your love for me all those months ago." He grinned and looked out to sea.

"Hey! You declared your love for me too. You haven't changed that much. You're just as lovely as you've always been."

"Not according to some people. Anyway, let's not talk about the past. I much prefer the present." He lifted her hand and kissed it. "Have I told you today how much I love you?"

"Only five times." Kira peered at the parcel again. "Is it a picnic? If it is, I don't know why you've wrapped it up like that. What kind of sandwiches have you made?"

"It's not a picnic. We'll be at the lighthouse soon. Be patient."

"I'm trying." The corner of her mouth twitched. "Perhaps I'd feel more patient if I held the package."

Ben laughed. "Nice try, but I'm not falling for that. You'd run off and unwrap it."

"What a thing to suggest! You know I don't run, not anymore. I would walk briskly away, and then unwrap it." Kira pulled on Ben's hand. "Come on, hurry up. We'll never get to the lighthouse at this rate!"

Kira tried to pull Ben along the coastal path, but it was like trying to move a brick wall. Ben refused to move at anything above a strolling rate.

A short while later, they arrived at the lighthouse. Kira sat on the bench and held her hands out, an expectant look on her face.

Ben sat at her side and put the parcel on his lap. He said, "You get a good view of my kiosk from up here. Daisy was right about extending it and adding an outdoor seating area."

"Daisy is always right." Kira wiggled her fingers and waggled her eyebrows. "I'm ready for my present now."

Ben carried on, "She was right about the website too. Who knew it would take off like that? And to think, our company now supplies ice cream to all the major supermarkets up and down the country. It's amazing."

"Yes, I know. I've been a part of it."

Ben gave her his full attention. "It's because of you that I've expanded my business. You've made me brave. You've made me want to be a better man, Kira."

Kira blinked as tears came to her eyes. "You've always been a good man."

"I'm not sure about that. I've been selfish and bad-tempered. But since we got together, my whole world has changed. It's like the brightness on my world has been turned up. Everything is richer." He leaned forward and kissed her. "And it's all because of you."

Kira wiped a tear away. "I feel the same way, Ben. When we kissed for the first time, it was like all the parts of my life were being turned until they clicked into the right places." She frowned. "I don't think I'm explaining it very well. It's like my life was good as it was, but when we got together, it was even better. Like you were the missing part in my jigsaw." She started to laugh. "Oh! I'm useless at trying to explain how I feel."

"Me too. That's why I've got you this." He placed the package in her hands. "You can open it now."

Kira gazed at the parcel. Her heart was suddenly beating too fast. Slowly, she unwrapped it and looked at the brightly coloured box beneath. She gave Ben a quizzical look and said, "You've got me a kaleidoscope?"

"I had it specially made for you. Take it out of the box."

Kira did so. She laughed when she saw the casing of the kaleidoscope was covered in images of ice creams.

"Look through it," Ben said gently.

Kira lifted the kaleidoscope up to her right eye and looked through it. She gasped as tiny blue butterflies filled the bottom part of the item. She slowly turned the bottom of the kaleidoscope which caused the butterflies to flutter around as if they were flying. Then a circle appeared in the middle of the butterflies. There was writing on it. Kira read it. Her heart missed a beat. She lowered the kaleidoscope and looked at Ben.

He smiled. "Did you read the message?"

Kira nodded silently.

"Well?" Ben asked nervously. "What's your answer? Will you marry me?"

Kira's eyes filled with tears once more. "Yes. Yes! Of course I will!"

Ben patted his chest. "Thank goodness for that! I've been holding my breath for the last minute. Open the top of the kaleidoscope."

Kira did so and found a beautiful diamond ring. She tried to pick it up but her hands were shaking too much. Ben picked it up and lovingly placed it on her finger.

Kira smiled at him. "I love you, Ben Roberts. I even love you more than ice cream."

Ben laughed. "That is good to know." He put his arm around her shoulders and pulled her close.

Kira's heart was full of joy and love. Her life was wonderful just as it was, and nothing needed to change. A holly blue butterfly landed at the side on the bench and flapped its wings gently as if in agreement.

A note from the author

I HOPE YOU ENJOYED this story. If you did, I'd love it if you could post a small review. Reviews really help authors to sell more books. Thank you!

This story has been checked for errors by myself and my team. If you spot anything we've missed, you can let us know by emailing us at: cathy@cathyblossom.com

---

WARM WISHES
Cathy Blossom

Other books by Cathy Blossom

HOLLY BLUE BAY SERIES:

BOOK 1 - A FRESH START In Holly Blue Bay - free with all ebook retailers
Book 2 - Kira's Kaleidoscope
Book 3 - A Secret Love Comes To Town
Book 4 - Meet Me On The Pier

BILLIONAIRE CLEAN ROMANCES:

THE BILLIONAIRE GUEST - A Billionaire Clean Romance - Book 1
The Billionaire Writer - A Billionaire Clean Romance - Book 2
The Billionaire Movie Star - A Billionaire Clean Romance - Book 3

Kira's Kaleidoscope
A Holly Blue Bay Romance
(Book 2)
By
Cathy Blossom
Copyright 2018 by Cathy Blossom
All rights reserved. No part of this publication may be reproduced in any form, electronically or mechanically without permission from the author.